BENNY AND PENNY IN

LIGHTS OUT!

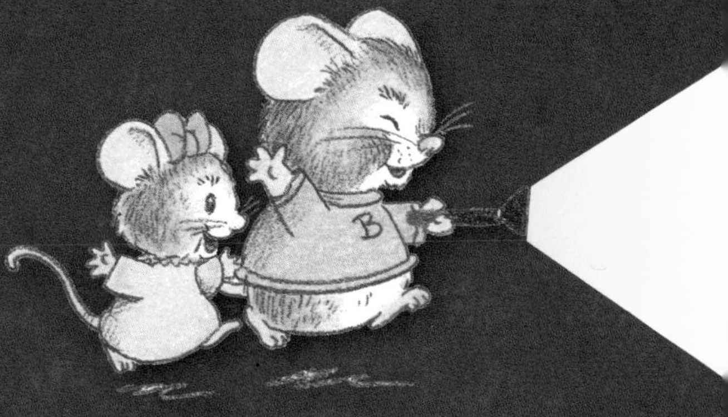

GEOFFREY HAYES

BENNY AND PENNY

IN

LIGHTS OUT!

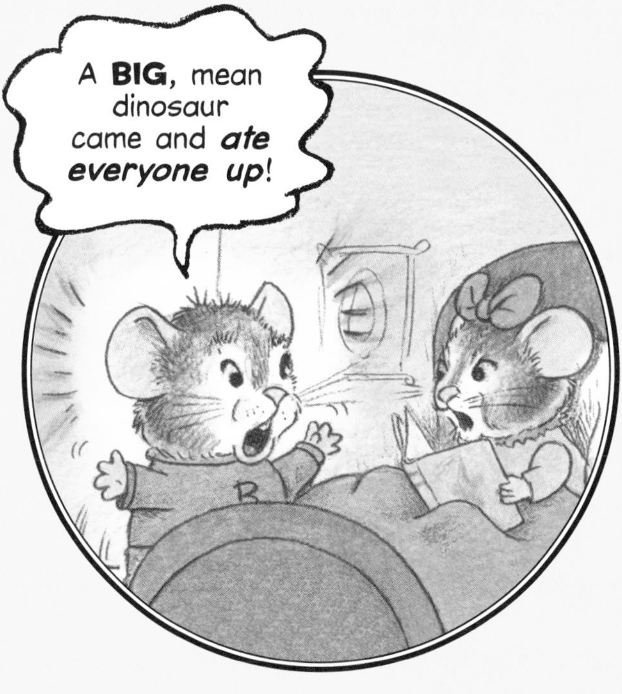
A **BIG**, mean dinosaur came and ***ate everyone up***!

A TOON BOOK BY

GEOFFREY HAYES

TOON BOOKS IS AN IMPRINT OF CANDLEWICK PRESS

A JUNIOR LIBRARY GUILD SELECTION
KIRKUS BEST CONTINUING SERIES:
Benny and Penny in Just Pretend
Benny and Penny in The Big No-No!
Benny and Penny in The Toy Breaker

For Pascual—a little night music!

Editorial Director: FRANÇOISE MOULY

Book Design: FRANÇOISE MOULY

GEOFFREY HAYES' artwork was drawn in colored pencil.

A TOON Book™ © 2012 Geoffrey Hayes & RAW Junior, LLC, 27 Greene Street, New York, NY 10013. TOON Books® is an
imprint of Candlewick Press, 99 Dover Street, Somerville, MA 02144. No part of this book may be used or reproduced in any
manner whatsoever without written permission except in the case of brief quotations embodied in critical articles and reviews.
TOON Books®, LITTLE LIT®, and TOON Into Reading™ are trademarks of RAW Junior, LLC. All rights reserved. Printed in
Singapore by Tien Wah Press (Pte.) Ltd.
Library of Congress Cataloging-in-Publication Data:
Hayes, Geoffrey.
Benny and Penny in Lights out! : a TOON book / by Geoffrey Hayes.   p. cm.
Summary: At bedtime two mouse siblings take turns telling stories and calming night fears.   ISBN 978-1-935179-20-7
1. Graphic novels. [1. Graphic novels. 2. Bedtime–Fiction. 3. Brothers and sisters–Fiction. 4. Mice–Fiction.] I. Title. II. Title: Lights out!
PZ7.7.H39Bc 2012   741.5'973–dc23   2011050927
ISBN 13: 978-1-935179-20-7 ISBN 10: 1-935179-20-9
12 13 14 15 16 17 TWP 10 9 8 7 6 5 4 3 2 1

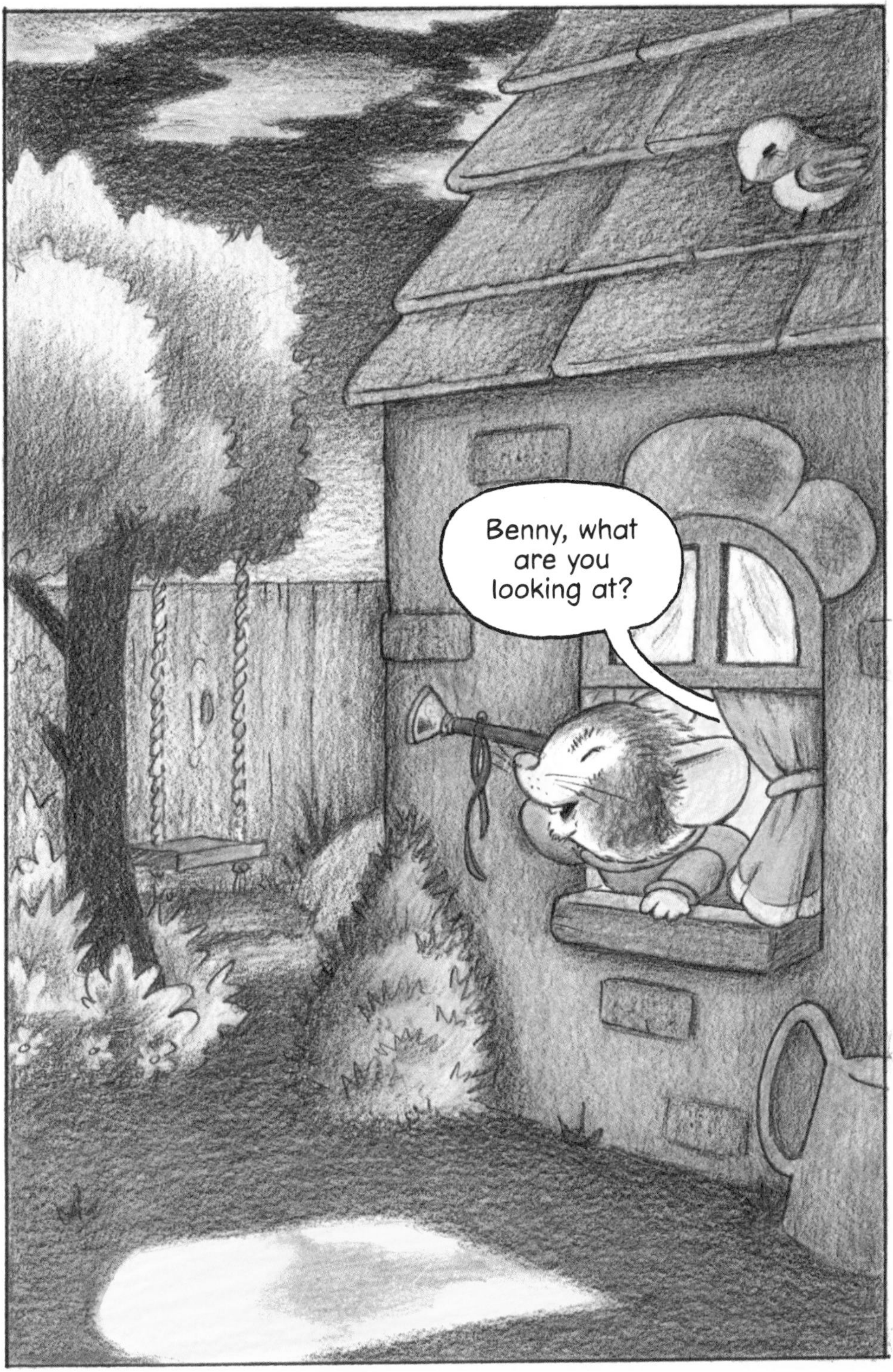
Benny, what are you looking at?

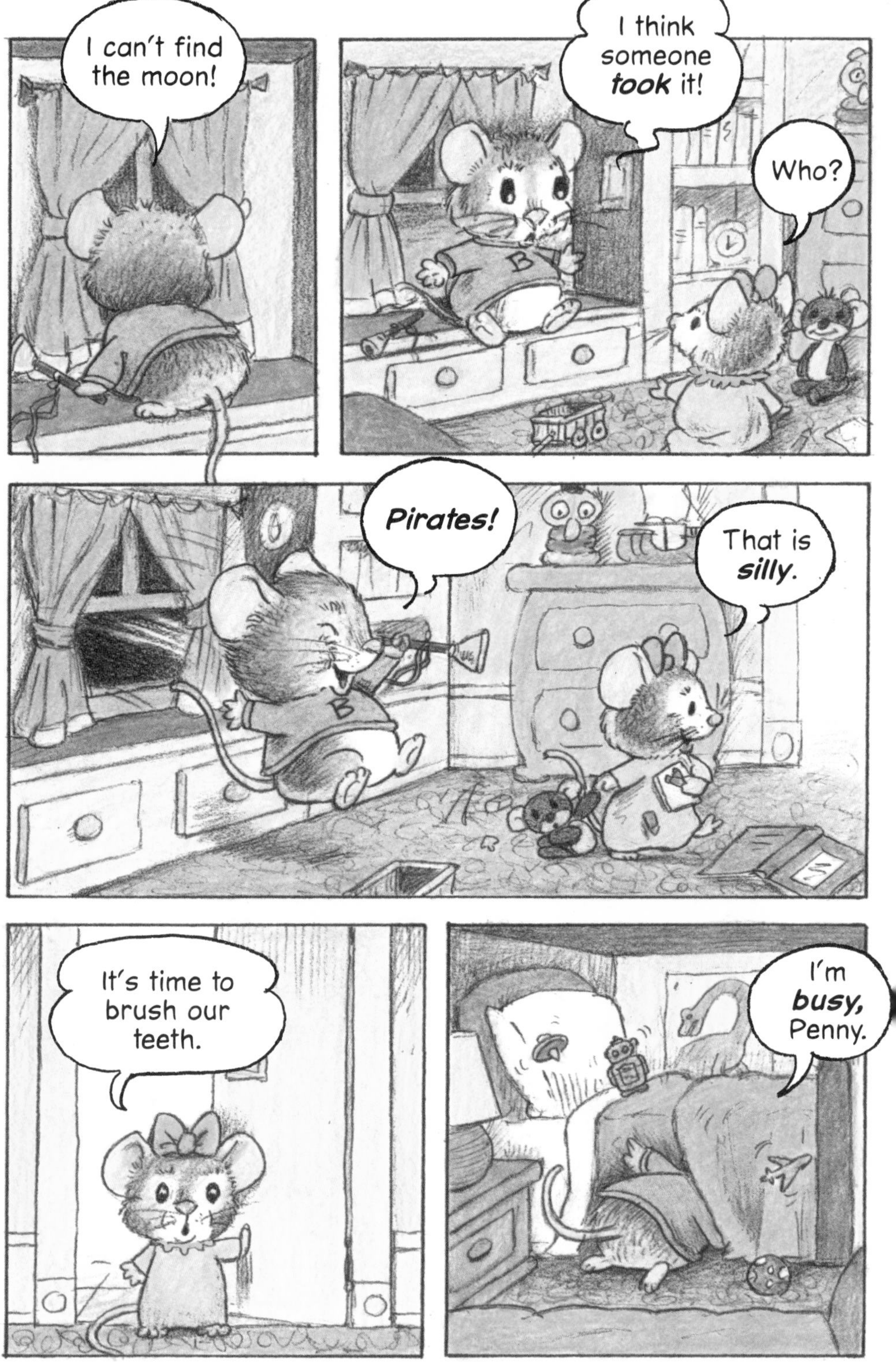
I can't find the moon!
I think someone *took* it!
Who?
Pirates!
That is *silly*.
It's time to brush our teeth.
I'm *busy,* Penny.

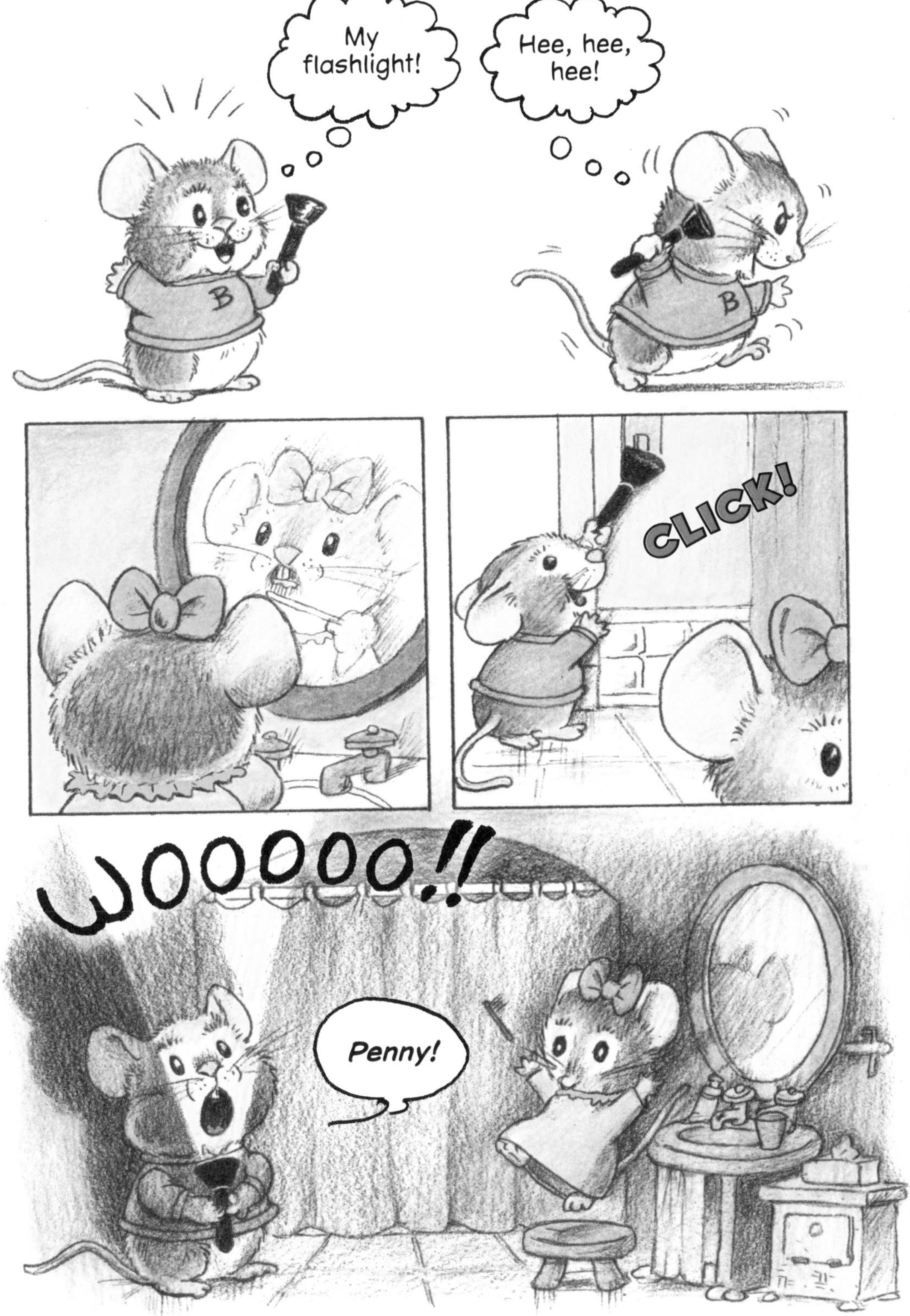
My flashlight!
Hee, hee, hee!
CLICK!
WOOOOO!!
Penny!

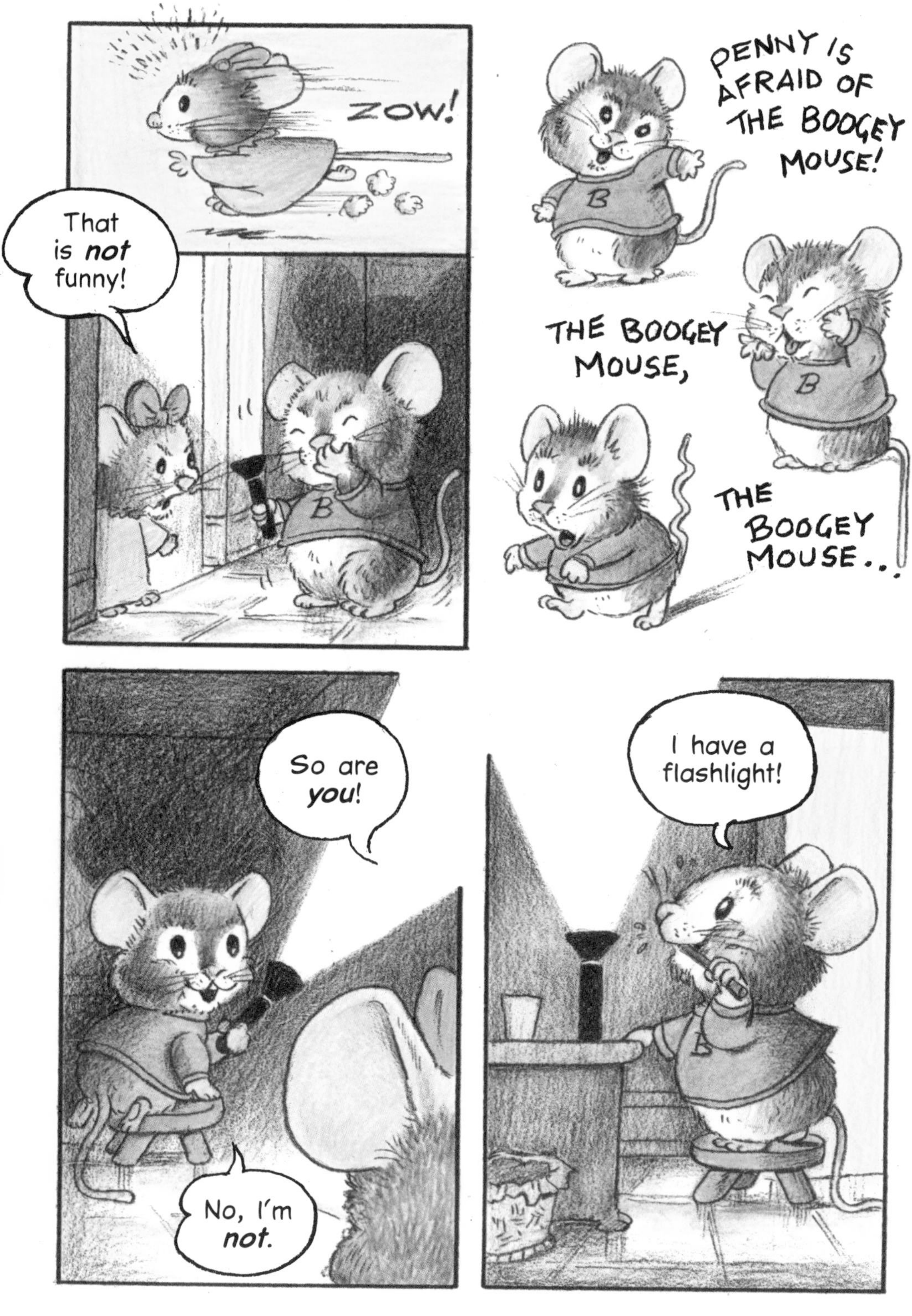
ZOW!
That is *not* funny!
PENNY IS AFRAID OF THE BOOGEY MOUSE!
THE BOOGEY MOUSE,
THE BOOGEY MOUSE..
So are *you*!
No, I'm *not*.
I have a flashlight!

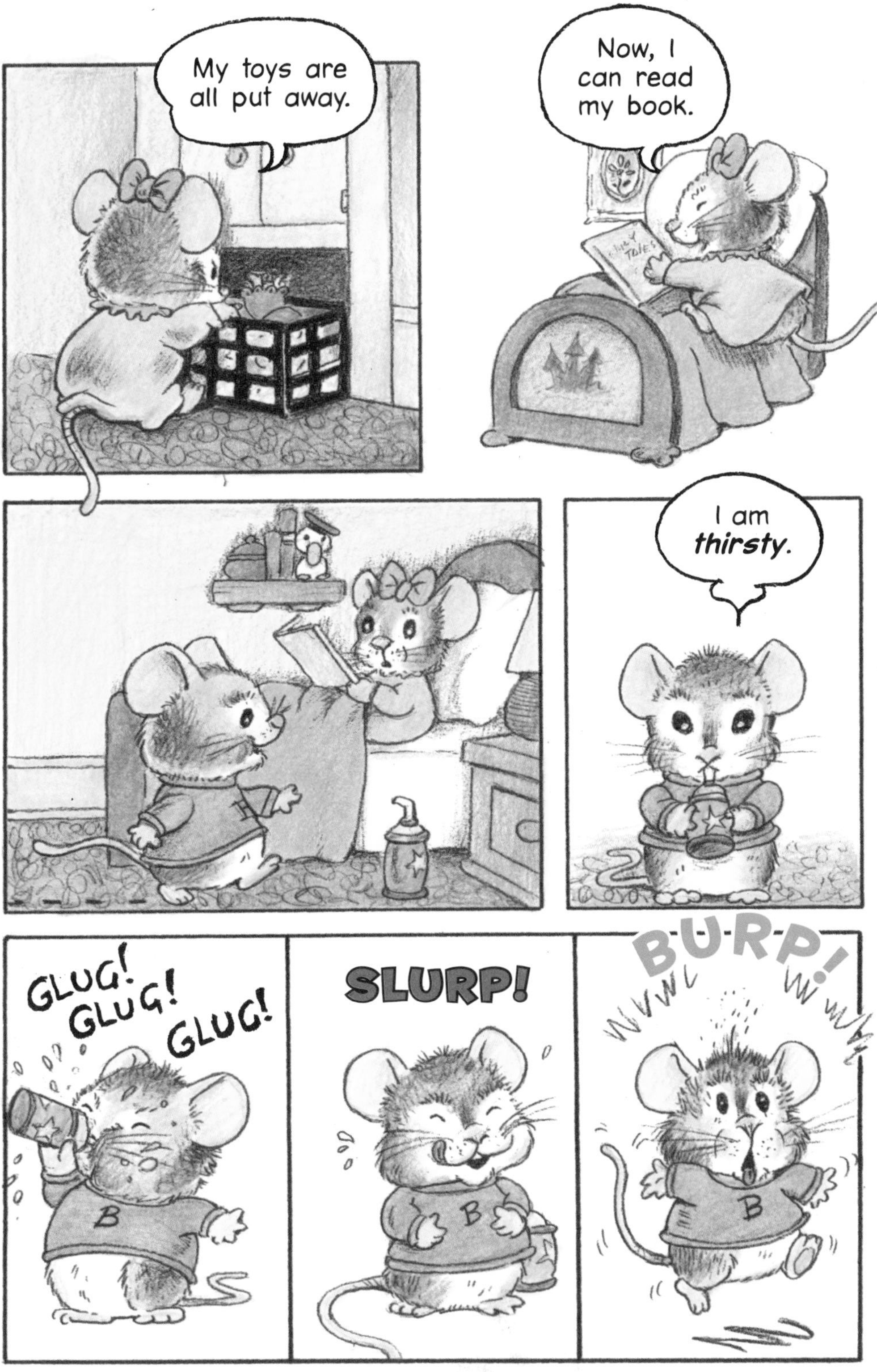
My toys are all put away.
Now, I can read my book.
I am *thirsty*.
GLUG! GLUG! GLUG!
SLURP!
BURP!

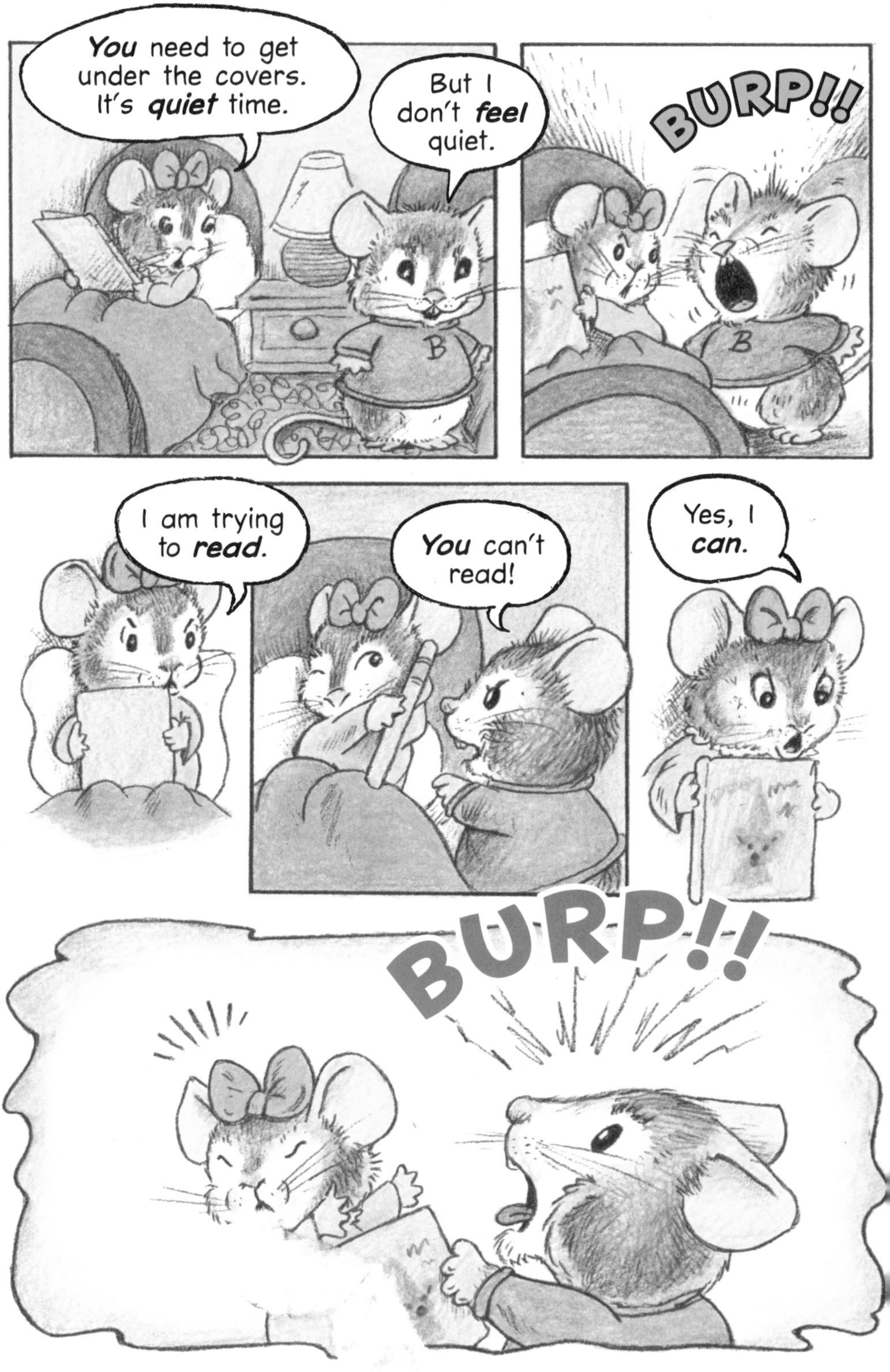
You need to get under the covers. It's quiet time.
But I don't feel quiet.
BURP!!
I am trying to read.
You can't read!
Yes, I can.
BURP!!

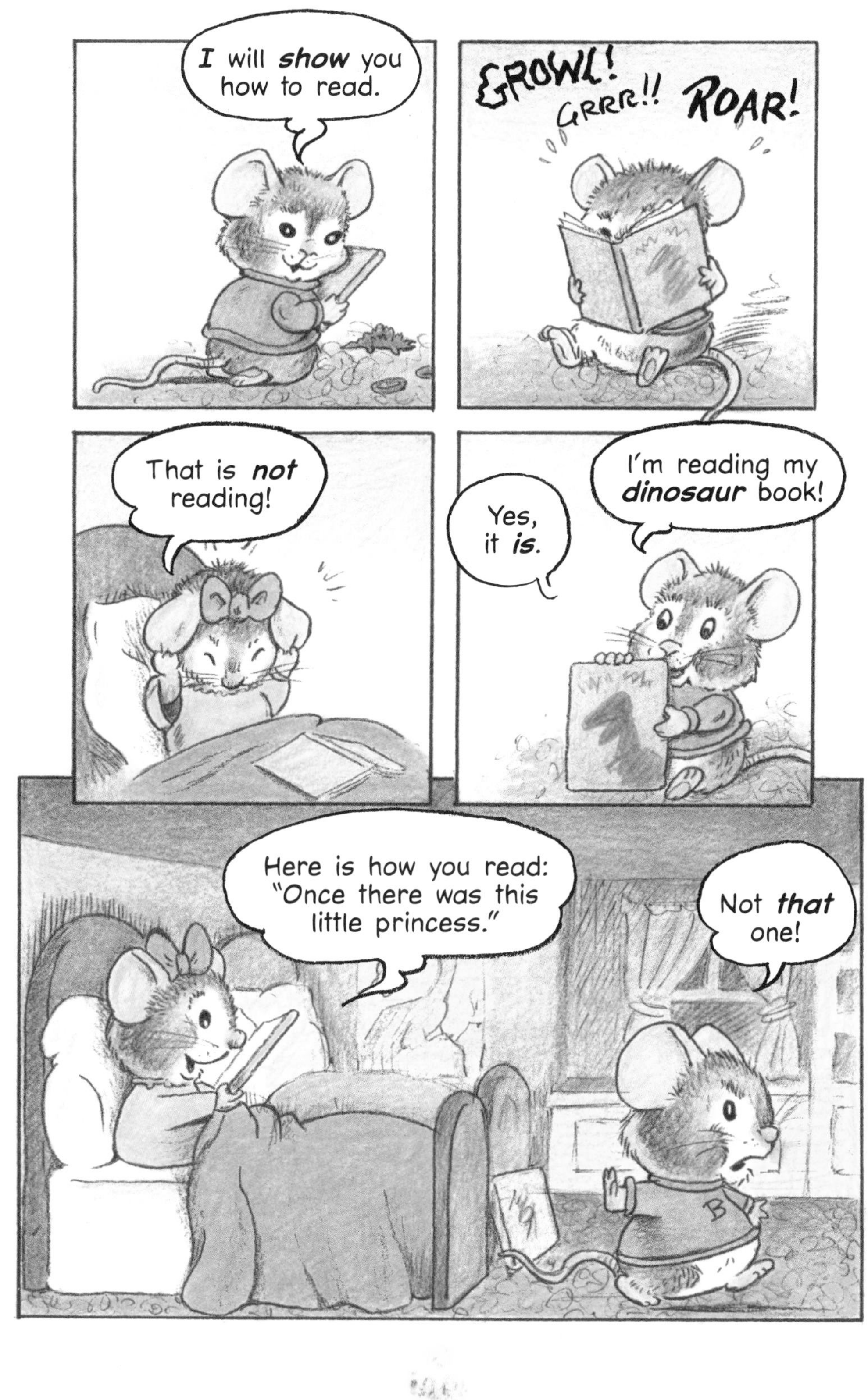

I will ***show*** you how to read.
GROWL!
GRRR!!
ROAR!
That is ***not*** reading!
Yes, it ***is***.
I'm reading my ***dinosaur*** book!
Here is how you read: "Once there was this little princess."
Not ***that*** one!

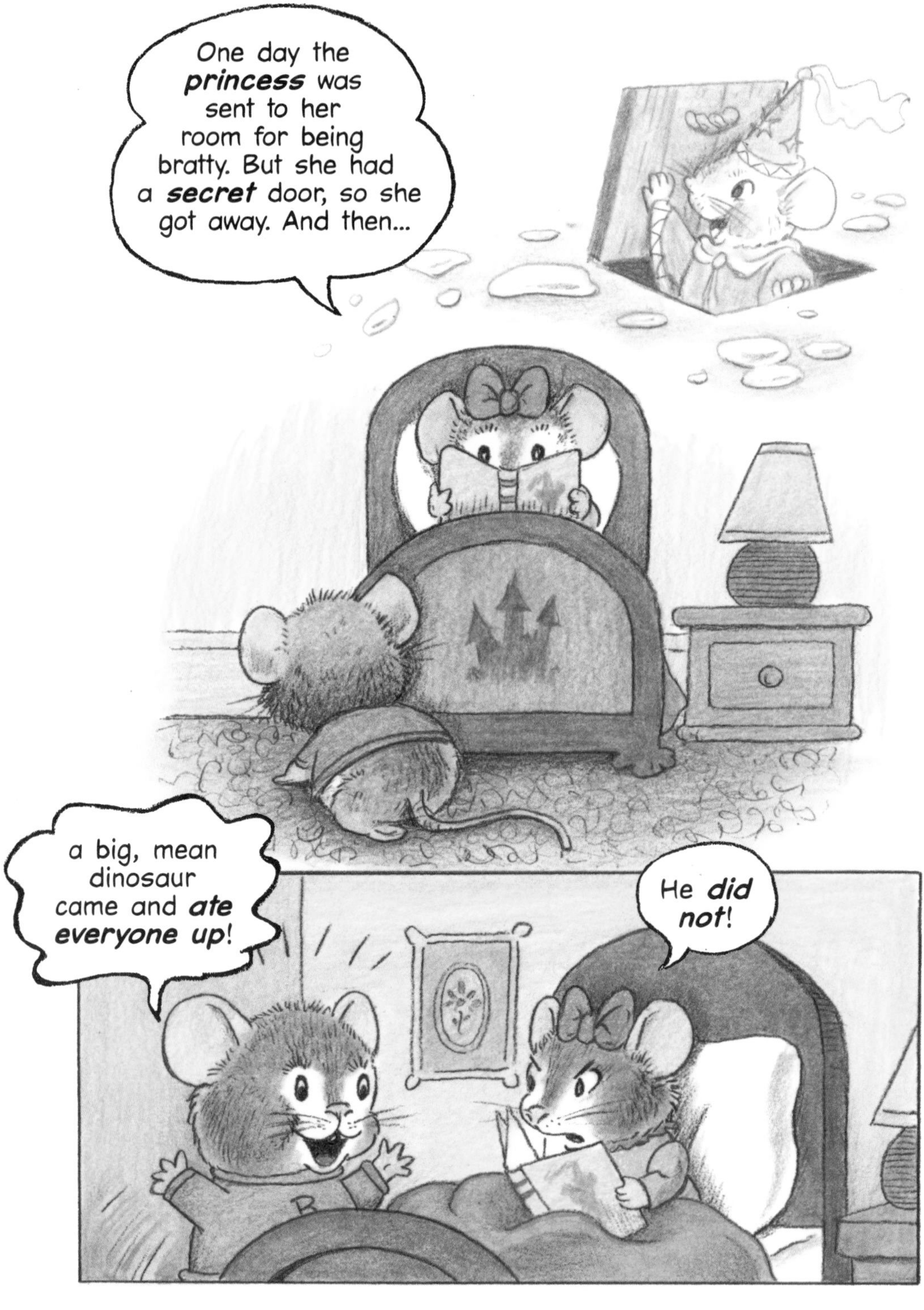
One day the ***princess*** was sent to her room for being bratty. But she had a ***secret*** door, so she got away. And then...
a big, mean dinosaur came and ***ate everyone up***!
He ***did not***!

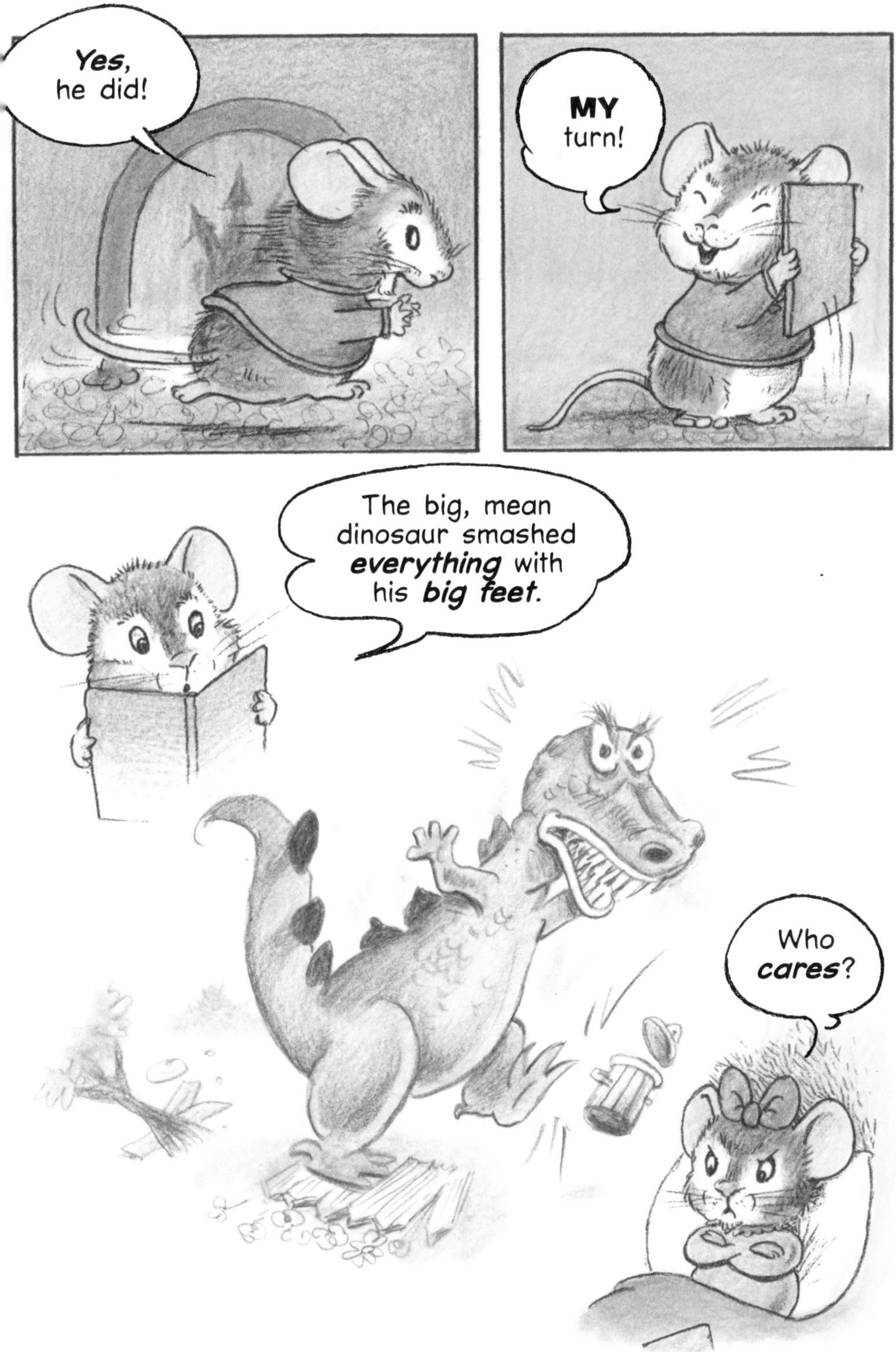
Yes, he did!
MY turn!
The big, mean dinosaur smashed ***everything*** with his ***big feet***.
Who ***cares***?

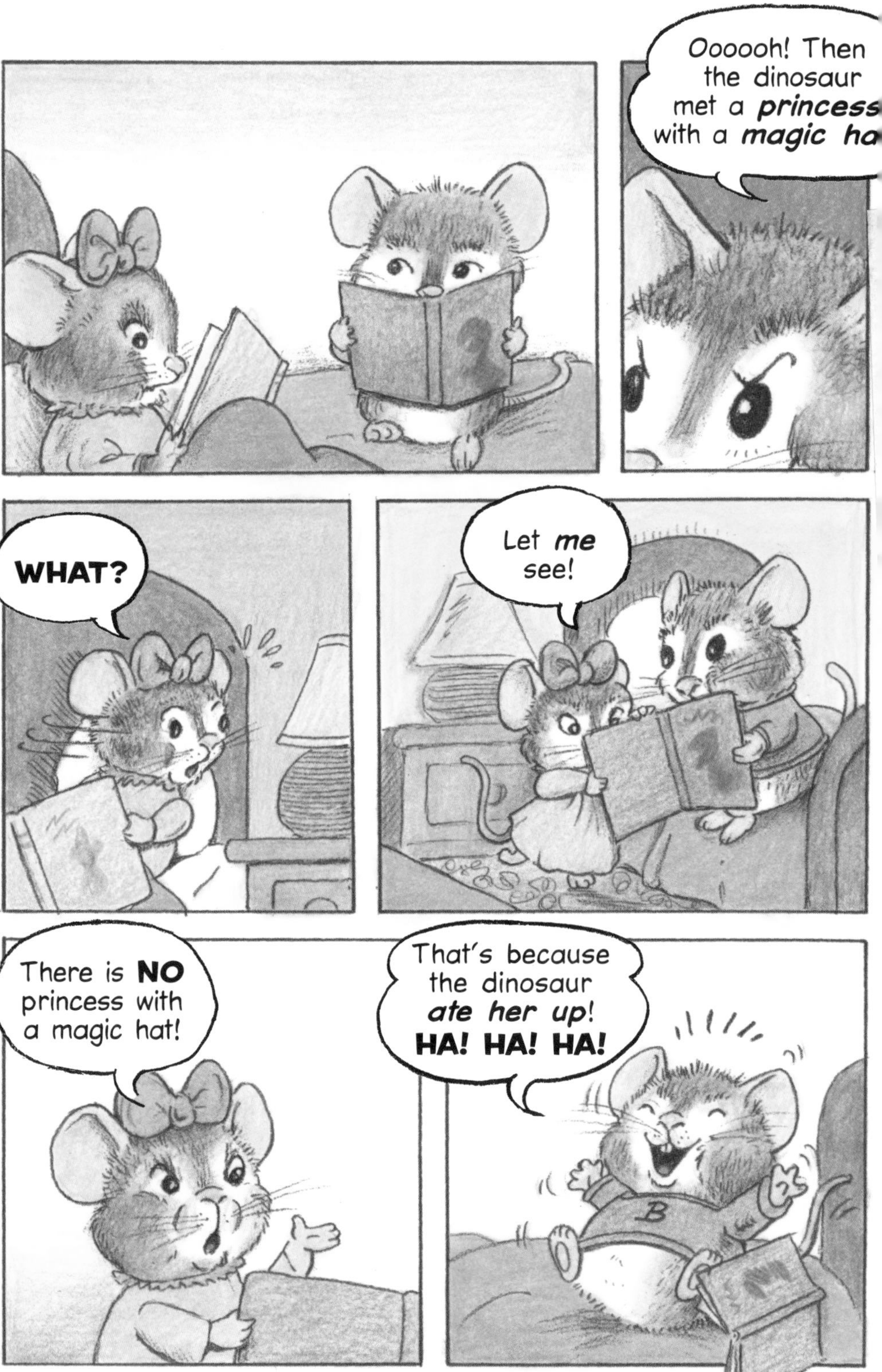
Oooooh! Then the dinosaur met a *princess* with a *magic* ha
WHAT?
Let *me* see!
There is **NO** princess with a magic hat!
That's because the dinosaur ***ate her up***! **HA! HA! HA!**

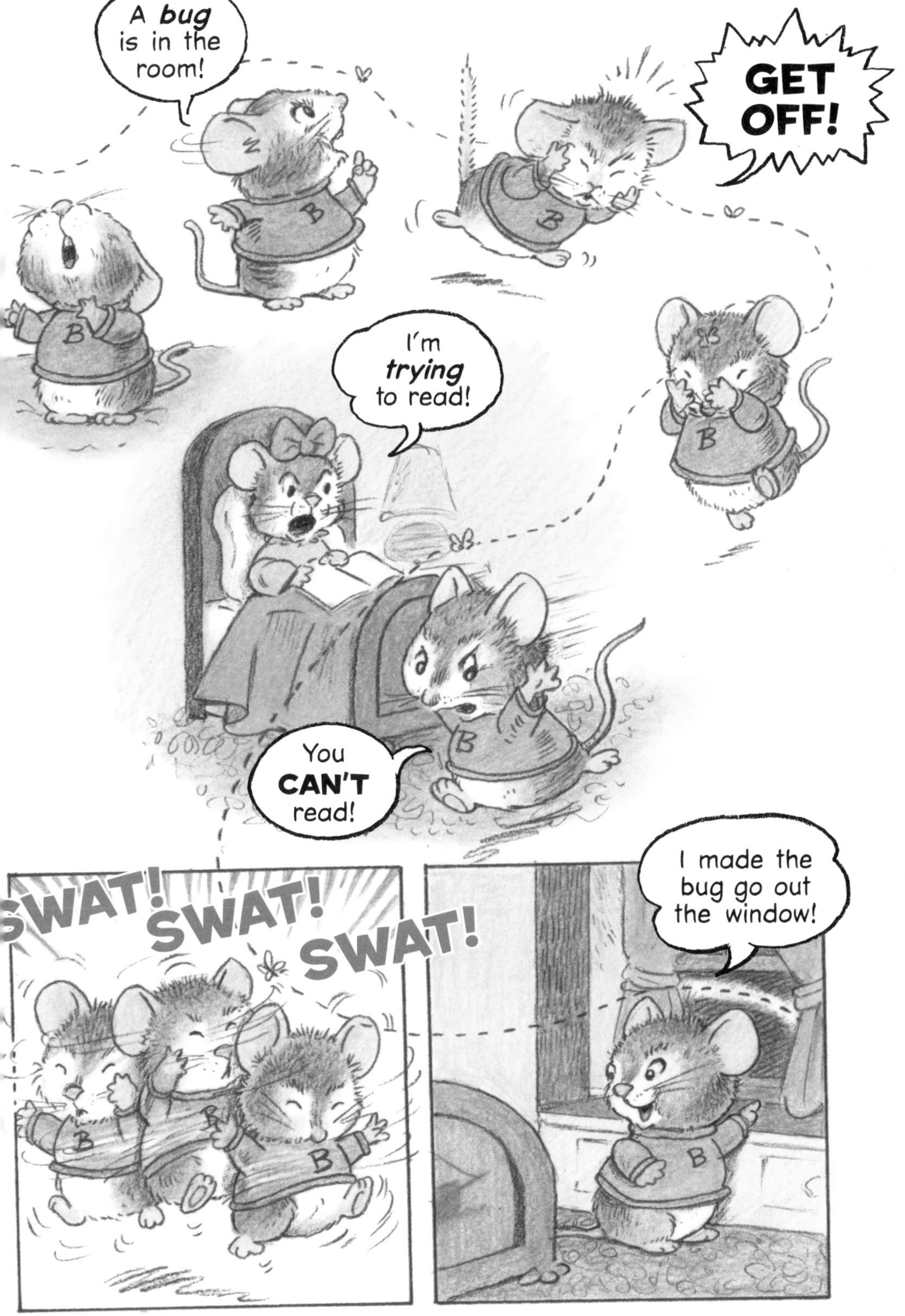
A *bug* is in the room!
GET OFF!
I'm *trying* to read!
You **CAN'T** read!
SWAT! SWAT! SWAT!
I made the bug go out the window!

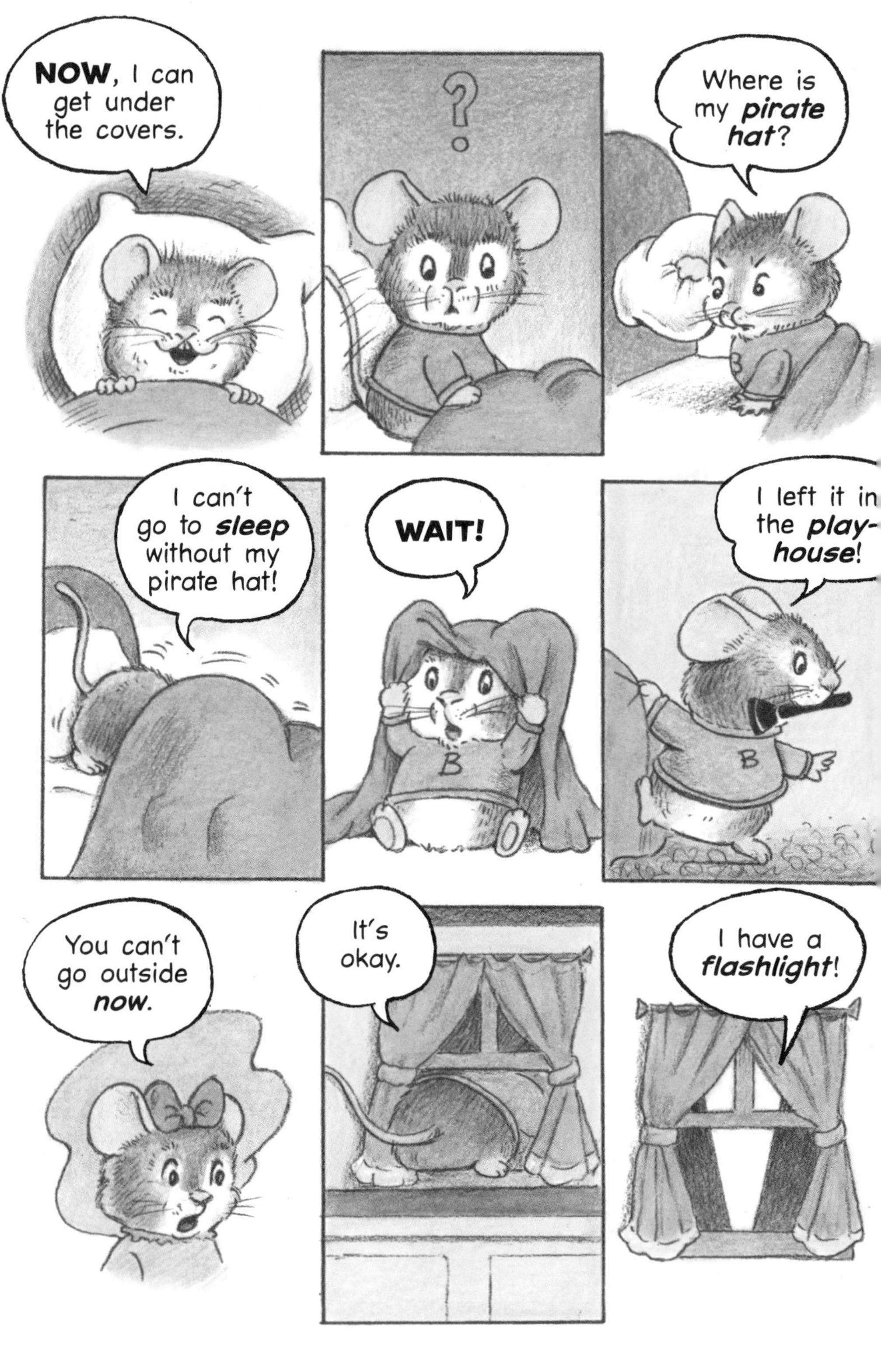
NOW, I can get under the covers.
?
Where is my pirate hat?
I can't go to sleep without my pirate hat!
WAIT!
I left it in the play-house!
B
You can't go outside now.
It's okay.
I have a flashlight!

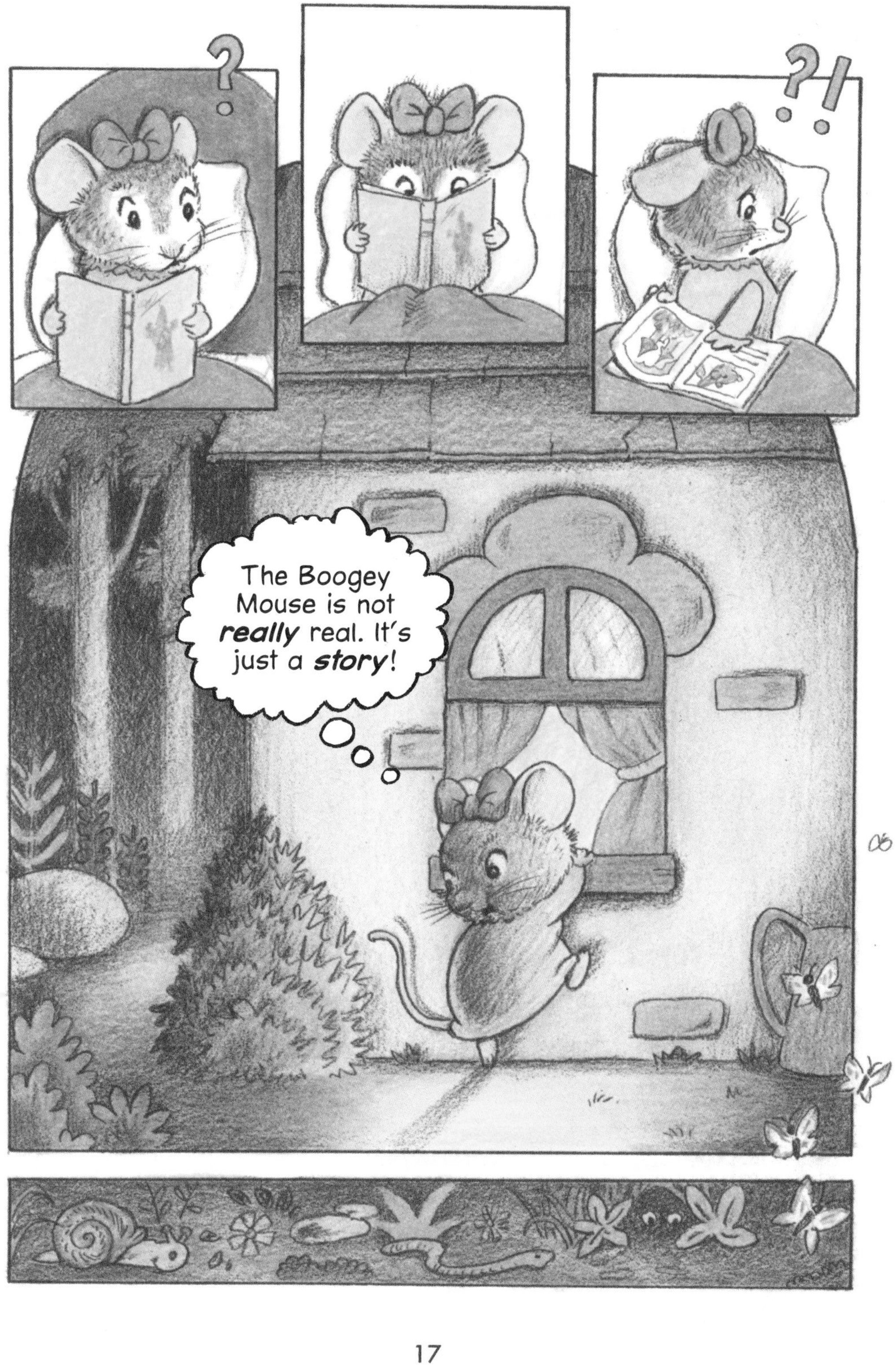
?
?!
The Boogey Mouse is not *really* real. It's just a *story*!

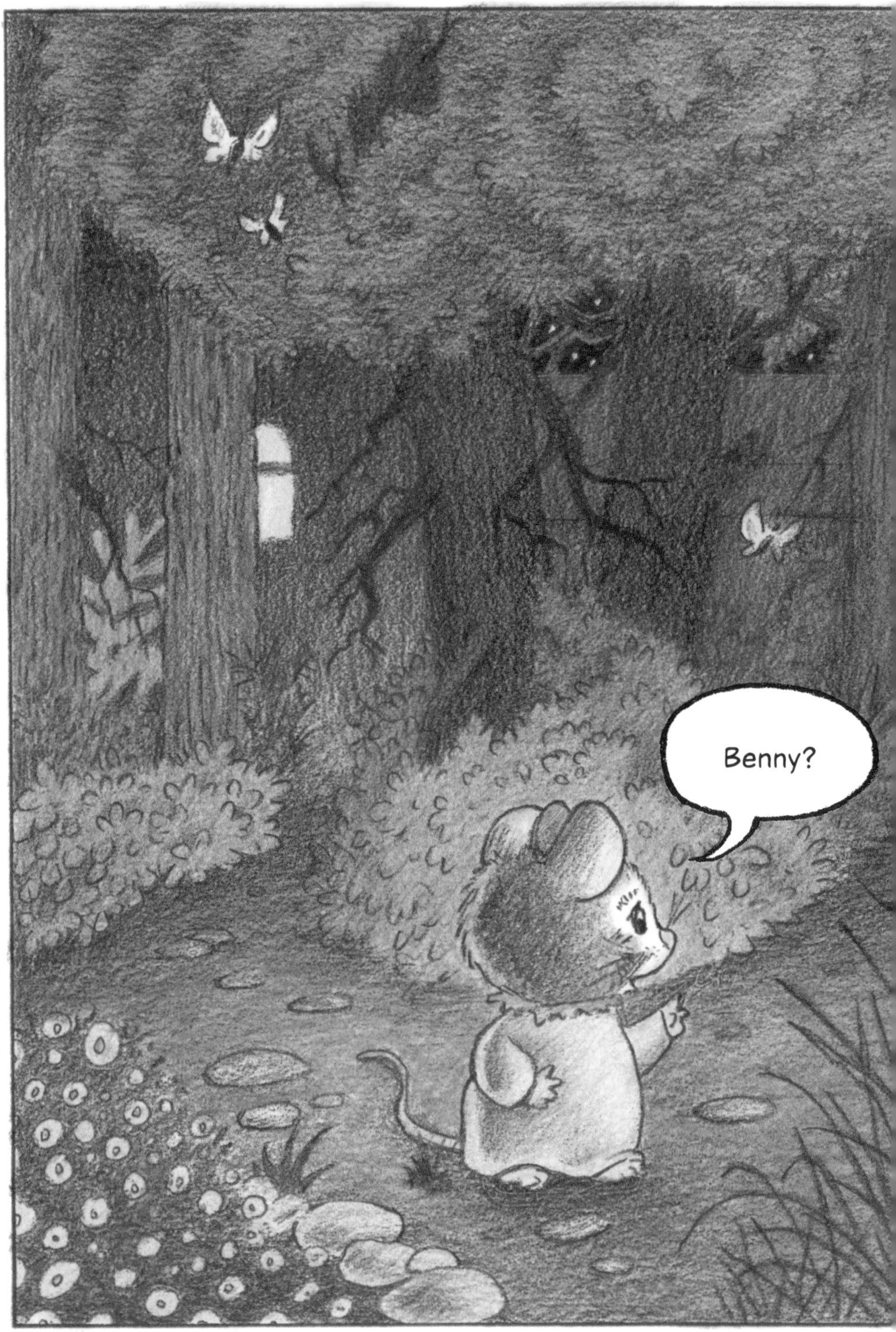
Benny?

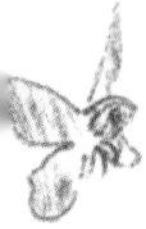

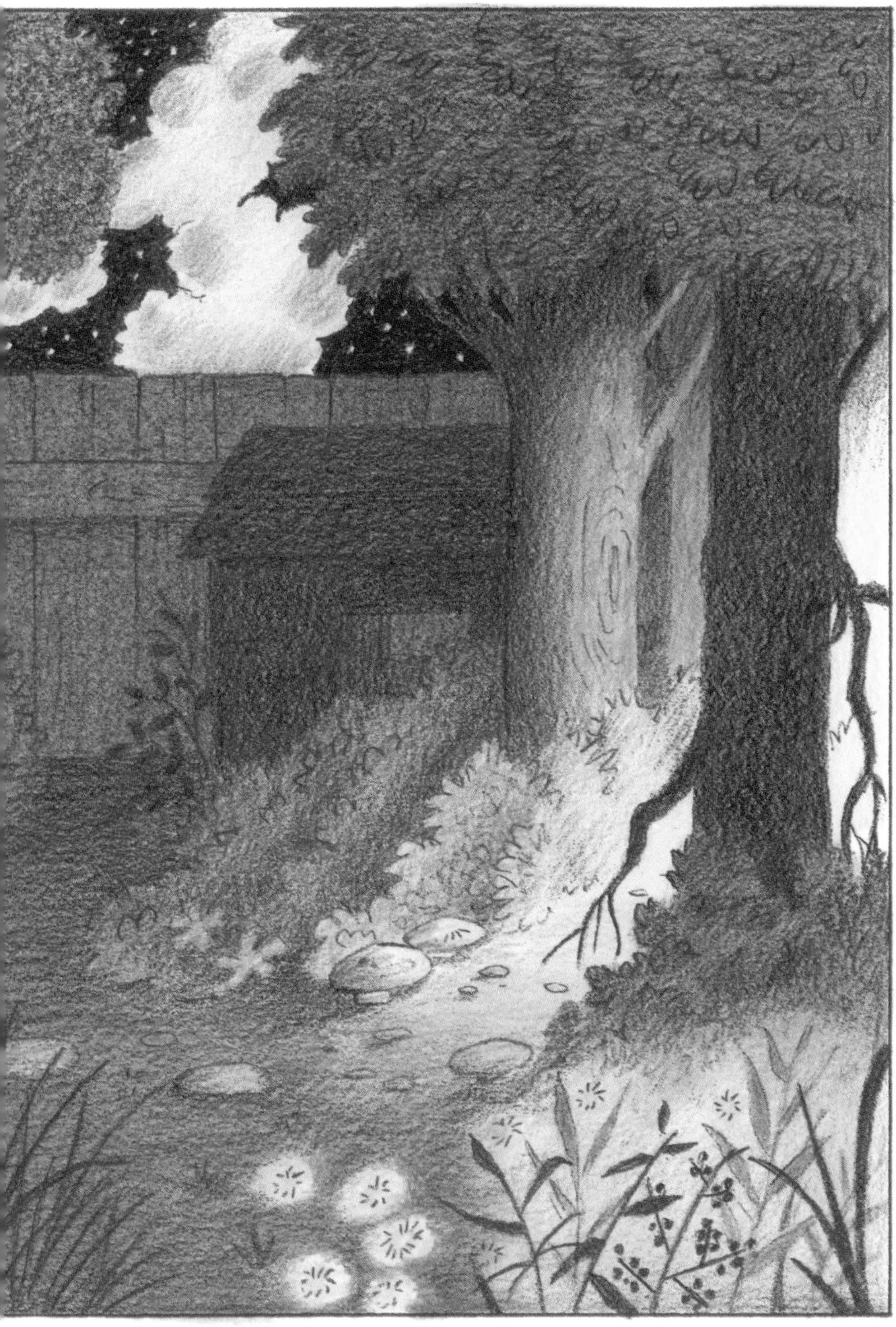

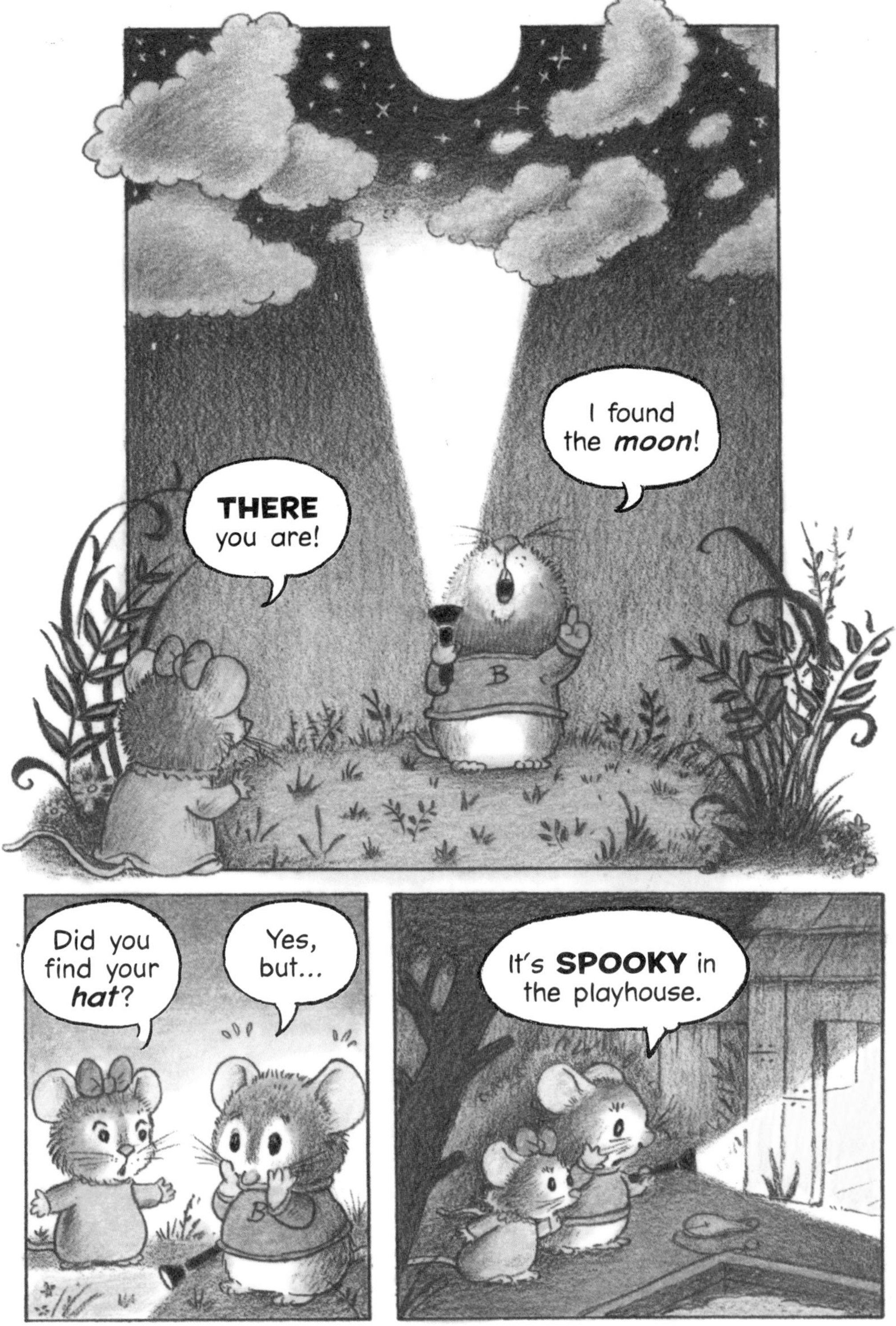
THERE you are!
I found the moon!
Did you find your hat?
Yes, but...
It's SPOOKY in the playhouse.

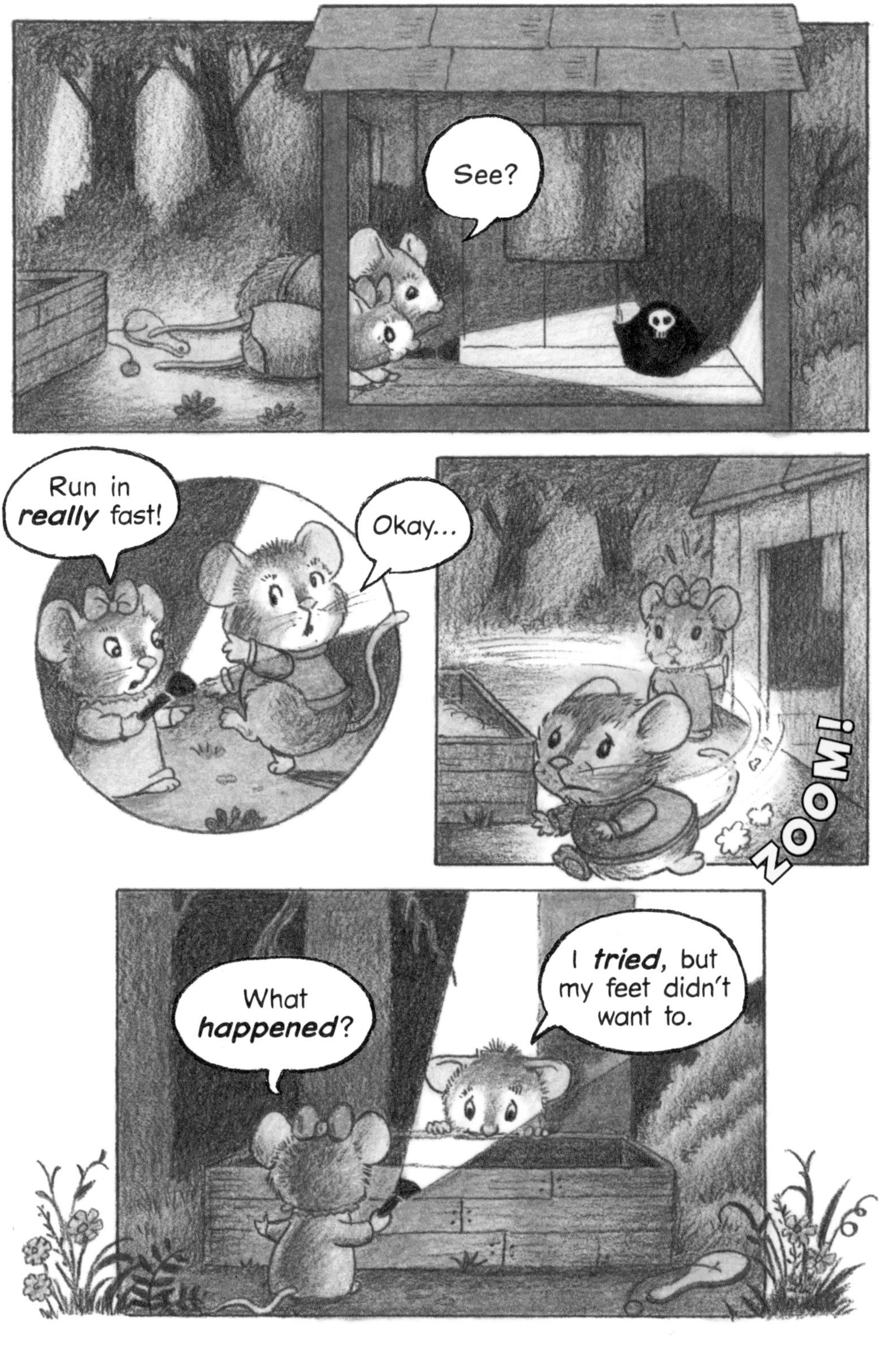
See?
Run in *really* fast!
Okay...
ZOOM!
What *happened*?
I *tried*, but my feet didn't want to.

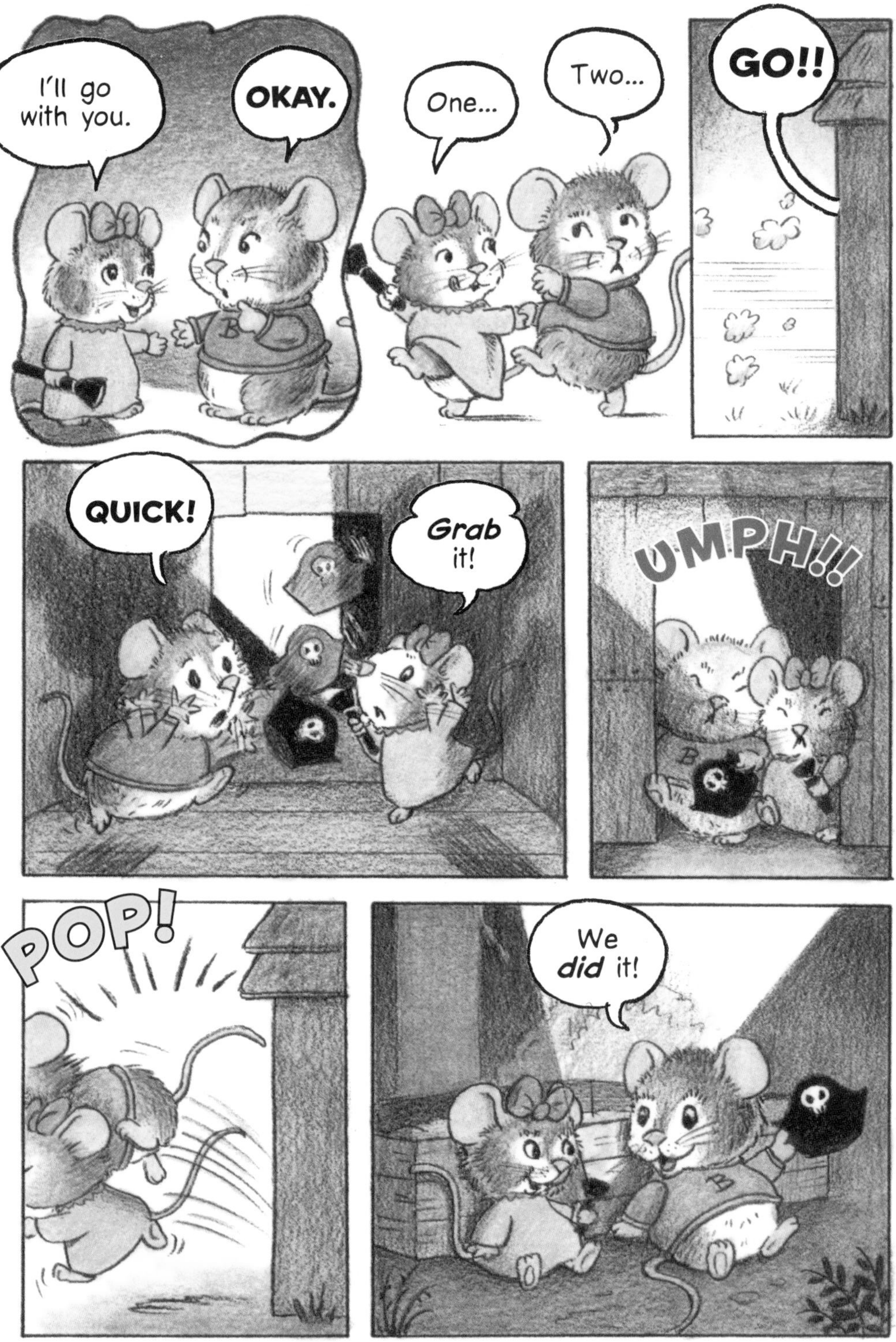
I'll go with you.
OKAY.
One...
Two...
GO!!
QUICK!
Grab it!
UMPH!!
POP!
We did it!

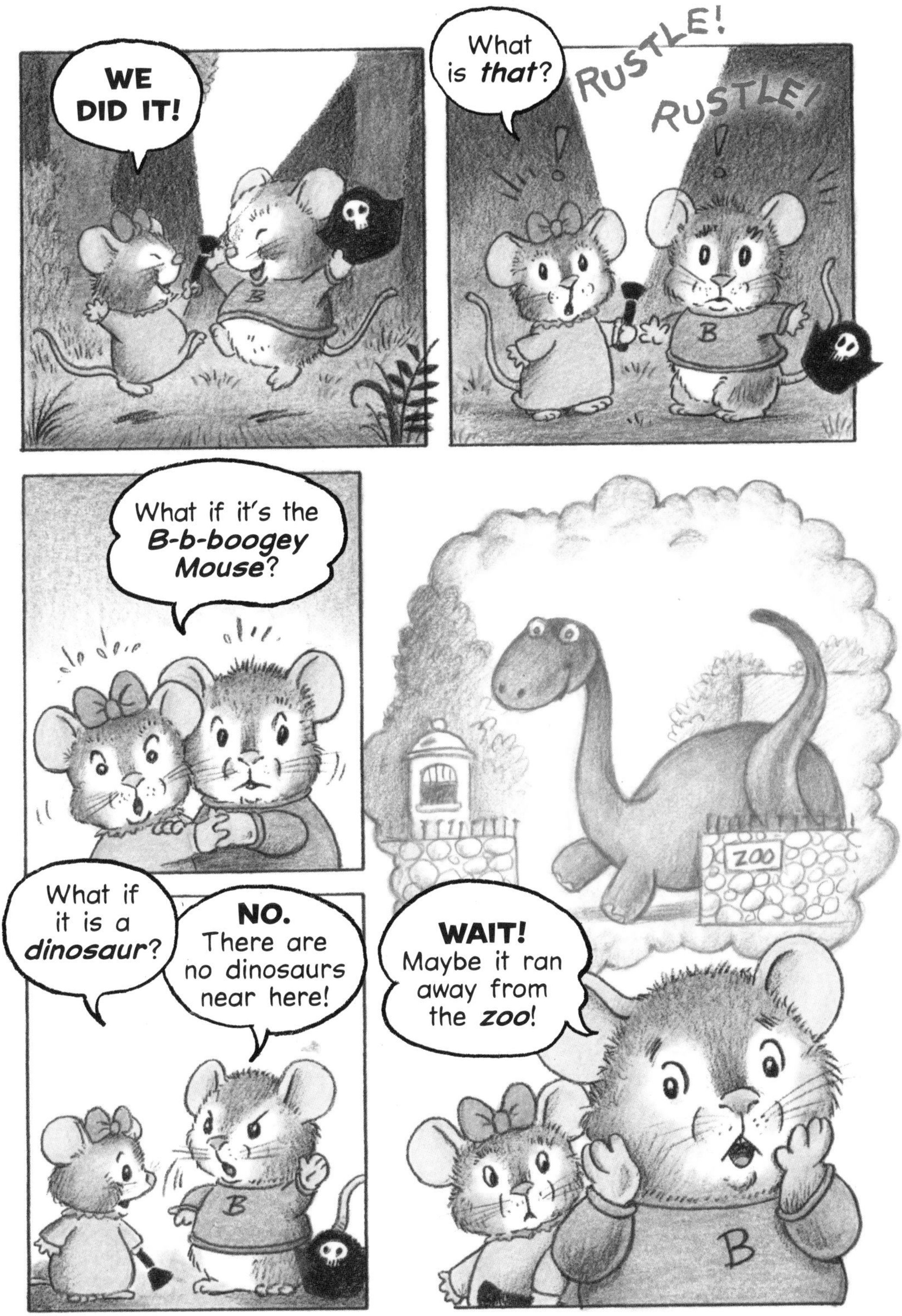

WE DID IT!
What is *that*?
RUSTLE!
RUSTLE!
What if it's the *B-b-boogey Mouse*?
ZOO
What if it is a *dinosaur*?
NO. There are no dinosaurs near here!
WAIT! Maybe it ran away from the *zoo*!

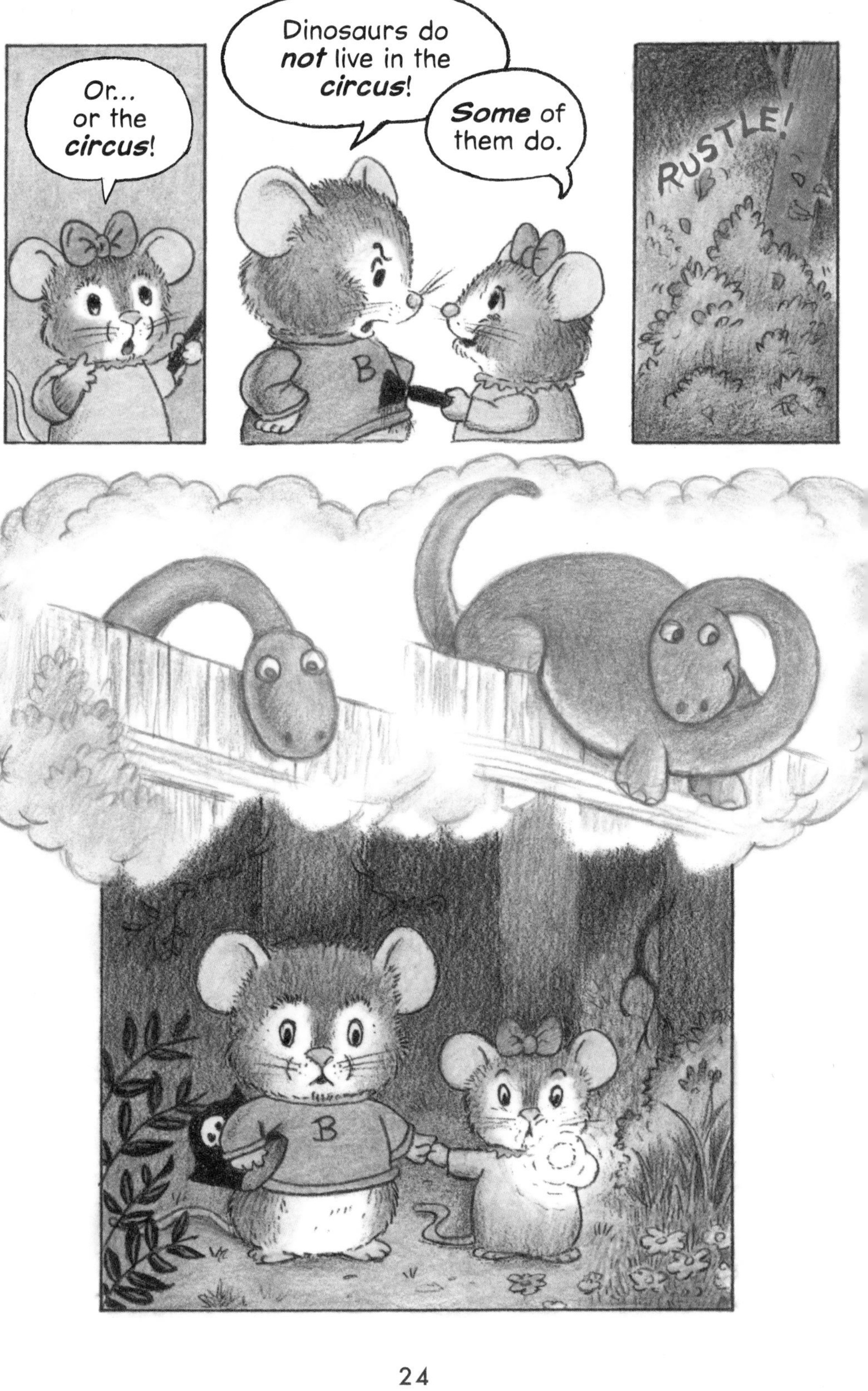
Or... or the *circus*!
Dinosaurs do *not* live in the *circus*!
Some of them do.
RUSTLE!

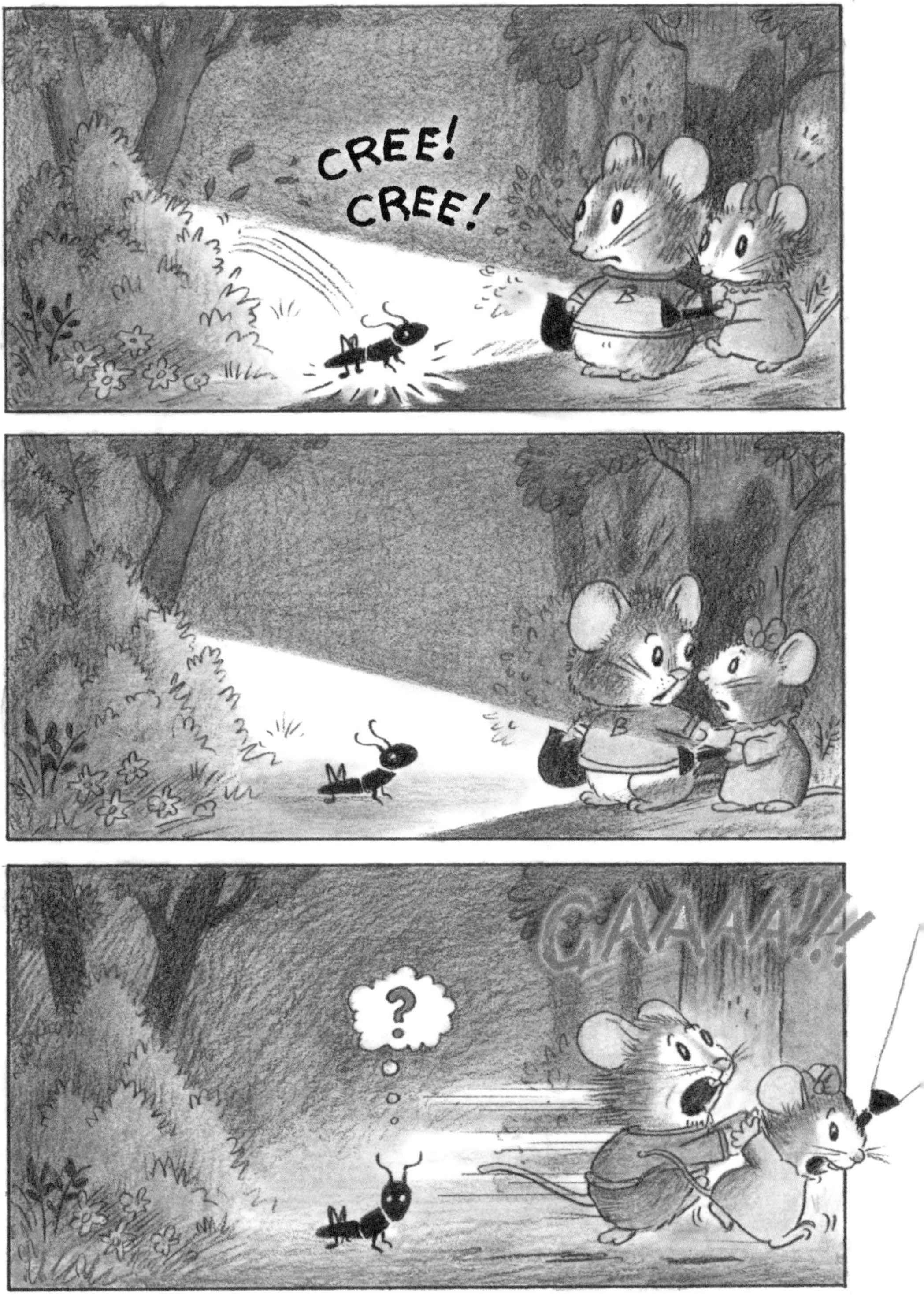
CREE!
CREE!
?
GAAAA!!!

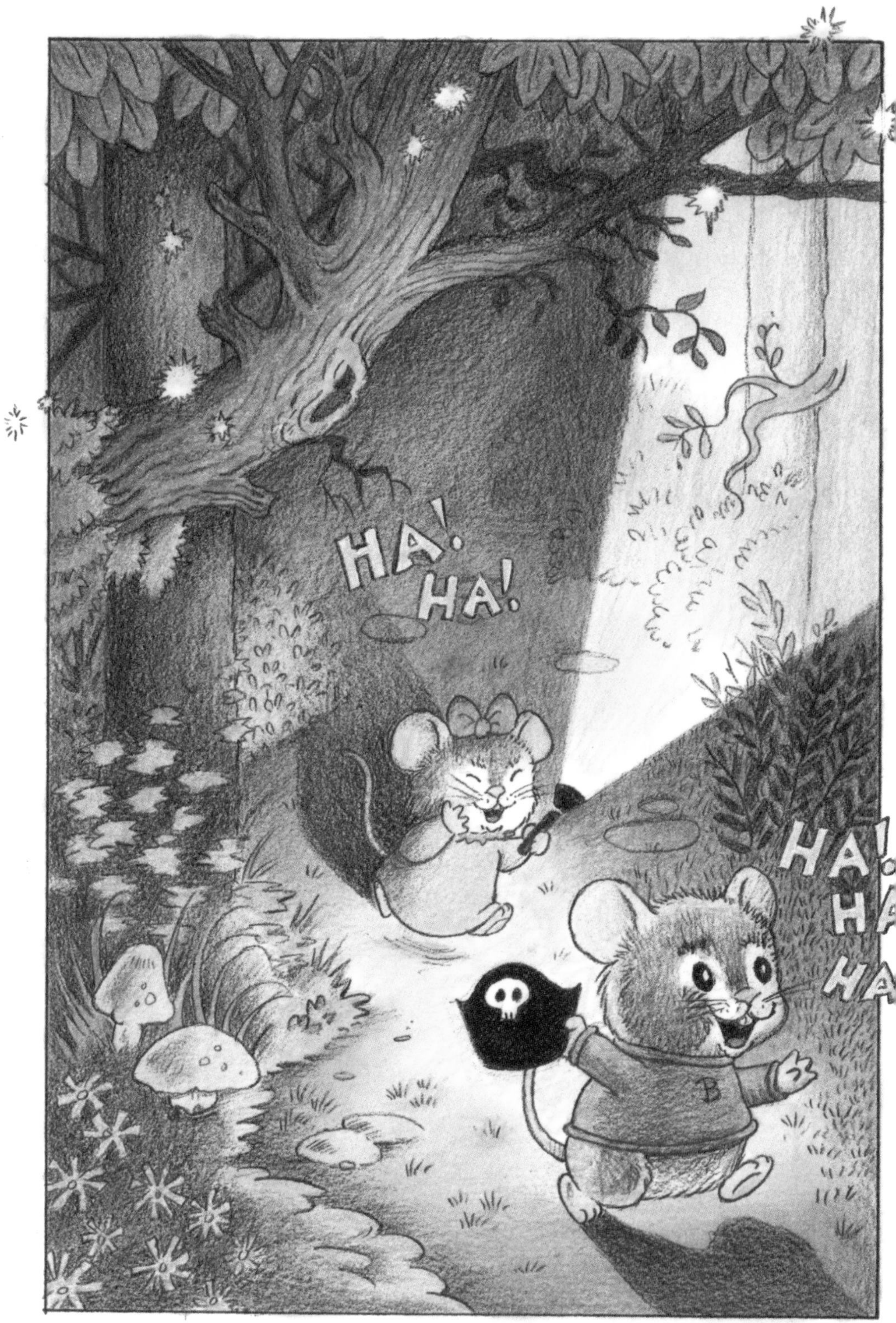
HA!
HA!
HA!
HA
HA

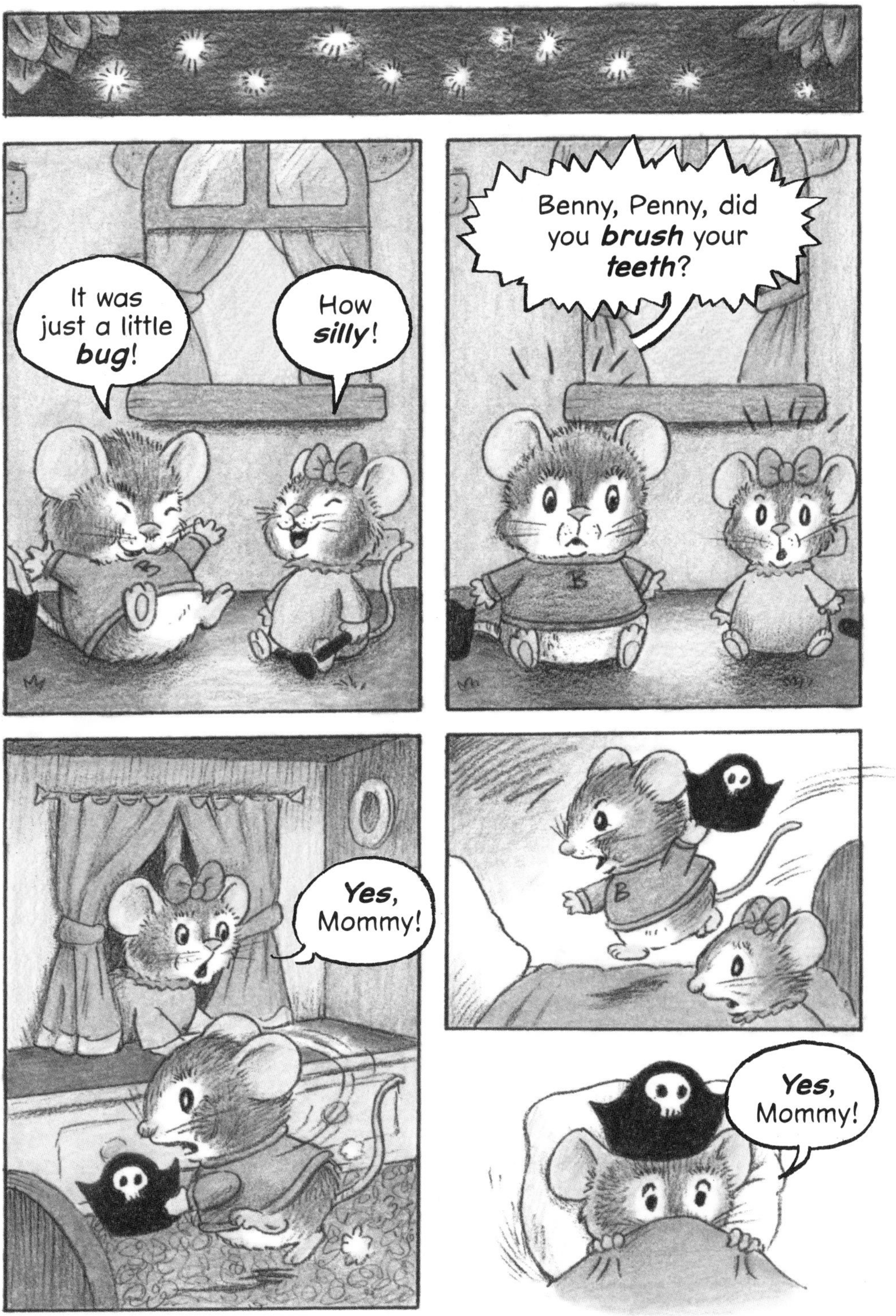
It was just a little **bug**!
How **silly**!
Benny, Penny, did you **brush** your **teeth**?
Yes, Mommy!
Yes, Mommy!

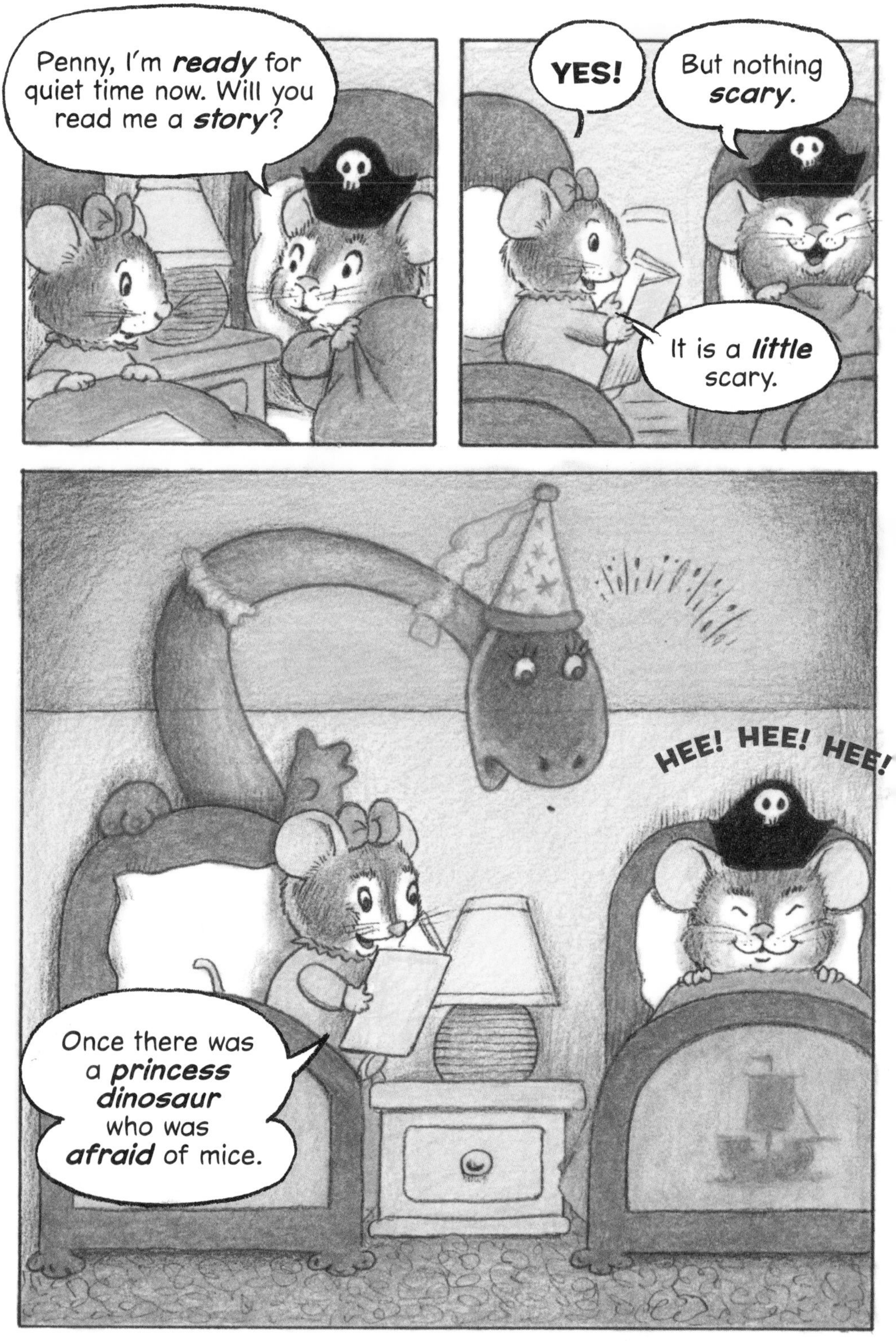
Penny, I'm **ready** for quiet time now. Will you read me a **story**?
YES!
But nothing **scary**.
It is a **little** scary.
HEE! HEE! HEE!
Once there was a **princess dinosaur** who was **afraid** of mice.

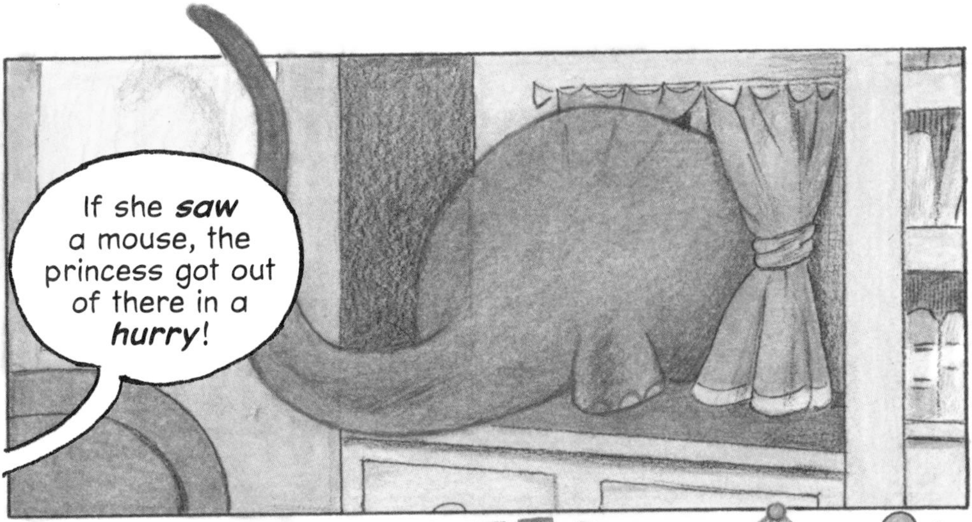
If she *saw* a mouse, the princess got out of there in a *hurry*!

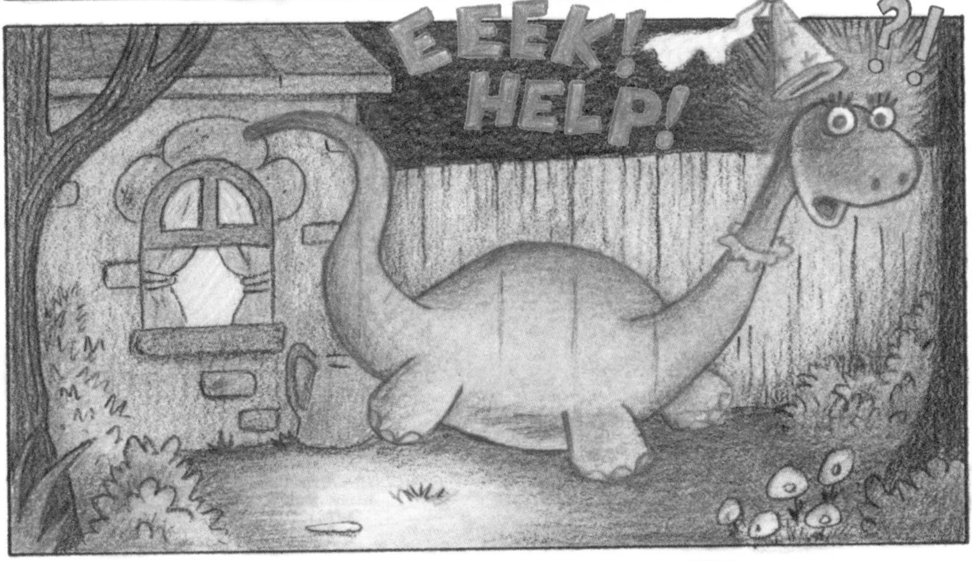
EEEK! HELP!
?!

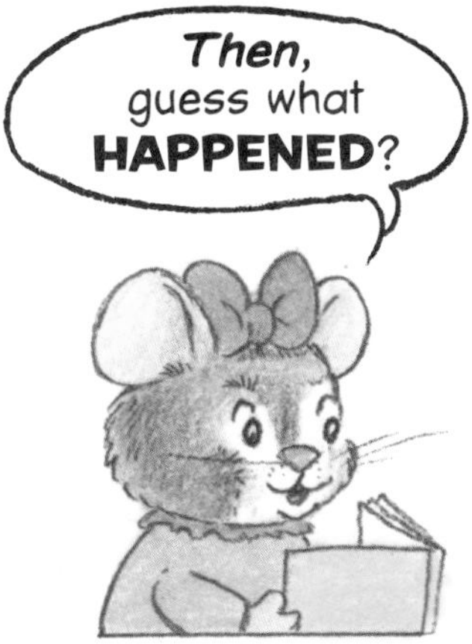
Then, guess what **HAPPENED**?

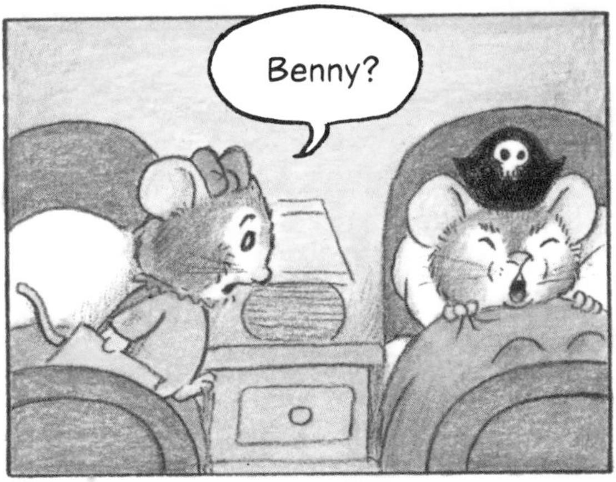
Benny?

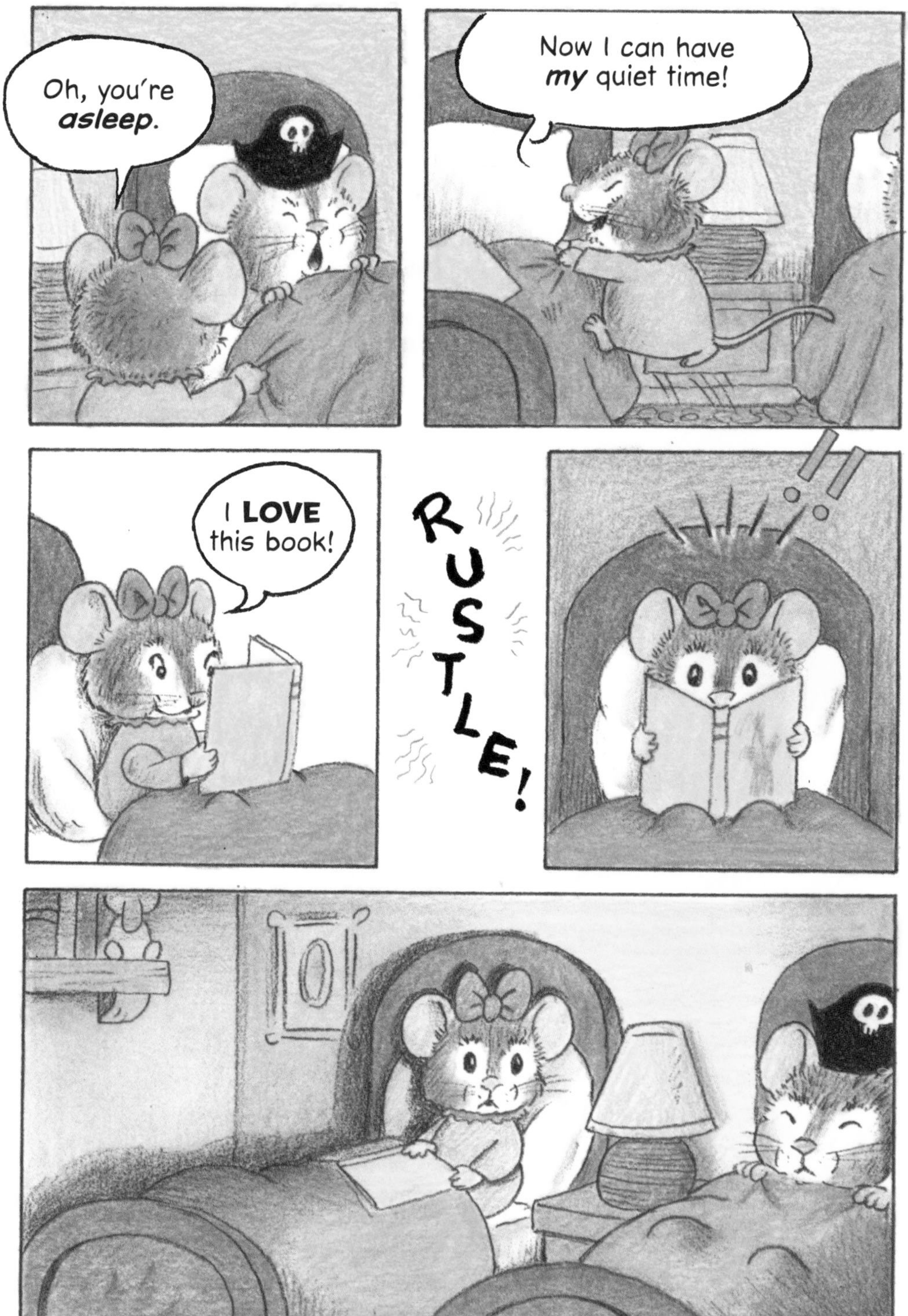
Oh, you're *asleep*.
Now I can have *my* quiet time!
I **LOVE** this book!
RUSTLE!
!!

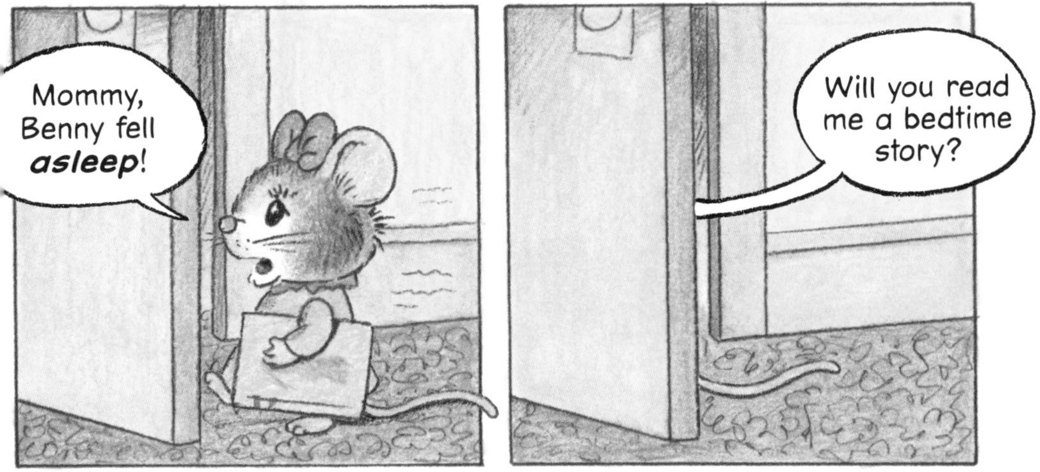
Mommy, Benny fell **asleep**!
Will you read me a bedtime story?

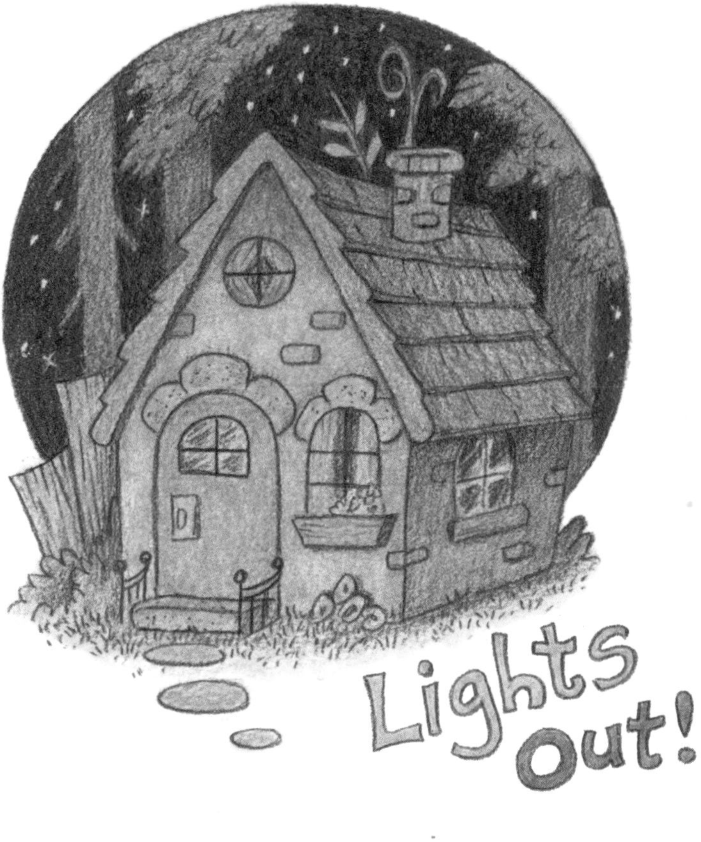
Lights out!

ABOUT THE AUTHOR

GEOFFREY HAYES has written and illustrated over forty children's books, including the extremely popular series of early readers *Otto and Uncle Tooth*, the classic *Bear by Himself*, and, most recently, *The Bunny's Night Light: A Glow-In-The-Dark Search*. His Benny and Penny titles for TOON Books are bestsellers and have garnered multiple awards. In 2010, *Benny and Penny in the Big No-No!* received the prestigious Theodor Seuss Geisel Award, given to the "most distinguished book for beginning readers published during the preceding year." When Geoffrey was younger, his flashlight was his favorite toy.

Geoffrey says, "My flashlight had red, green and blue filters that could be turned to change the color of the light. I used it to put on puppet plays starring my stuffed animals."

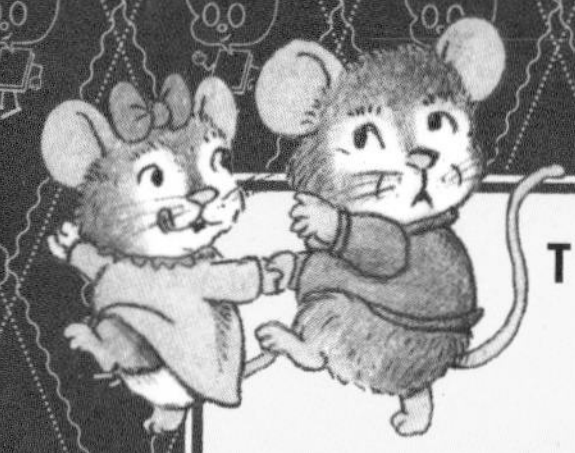

TIPS FOR PARENTS AND TEACHERS:

HOW TO READ COMICS WITH KIDS

Kids *love* comics! They are naturally drawn to the details in the pictures, which make them want to read the words. Comics beg for repeated readings and let both emerging and reluctant readers enjoy complex stories with a rich vocabulary. But since comics have their own grammar, here are a few tips for reading them with kids:

GUIDE YOUNG READERS: Use your finger to show your place in the text, but keep it at the bottom of the speaking character so it doesn't hide the very important facial expressions.

HAM IT UP! Think of the comic book story as a play and don't hesitate to read with expression and intonation. Assign parts or get kids to supply the sound effects, a great way to reinforce phonics skills.

LET THEM GUESS. Comics provide lots of context for the words, so emerging readers can make informed guesses. Like jigsaw puzzles, comics ask readers to make connections, so check a young audience's understanding by asking, "What's this character thinking?" (but don't be surprised if a kid finds some of the comics' subtle details faster than you).

TALK ABOUT THE PICTURES. Point out how the artist paces the story with pauses (silent panels) or speeded-up action (a burst of short panels). Discuss how the size and shape of the panels carry meaning.

ABOVE ALL, ENJOY! There is of course never one right way to read, so go for the shared pleasure. Once children make the story happen in their imagination, they have discovered the thrill of reading, and you won't be able to stop them. At that point, just go get them more books, and more comics.

www.TOON-BOOKS.com

SEE OUR FREE ONLINE CARTOON MAKERS, LESSON PLANS, AND MUCH MORE.

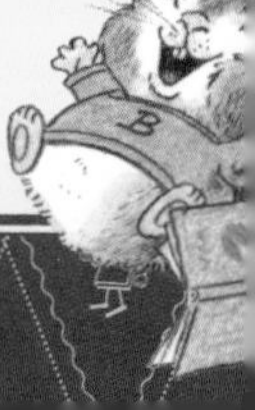